THE BURNING LAND

JOHN HUNTER

SAGEBRUSH
Large Print Westerns

First published in Great Britain by Gold Lion
First published in the United States by Ballantine

First Isis Edition
published 2021
by arrangement with
Golden West Literary Agency

A catalogue record for this book is available
from the British Library.

ISBN 978–1–78541–867–9

Published by
Ulverscroft Limited
Anstey, Leicestershire

Set by Words & Graphics Ltd.
Anstey, Leicestershire
Printed and bound in Great Britain by
TJ Books Ltd., Padstow, Cornwall

CHAPTER
ONE

In the bright silver bath of moonlight the rolling land through which the stage road twisted looked soft and gentle. It was not. It was dry, cruel country for many miles in every direction, flat land interrupted by the hills the stage was crossing and another range on the far side of Snakeshead Valley. The two areas of high ground pinched in close together further down, and through the wide gap the Whitewater River sluiced in a churning froth. Except for the river the whole territory was arid, a burning inferno in summer, a wind-blasted hell in winter.

The river made the difference. No matter how barren the earth appeared, given the miracle of water it would be transformed into a green, productive paradise. Water had controlled the development of the section from the first and it would now reshape the future of these hills and the vast flatlands to the south.

Cal Bentley watched the passing landscape and envisioned what it would look like within a few years. He had spent two weeks in the Territorial capital and he carried in his small traveling case the basic plans for the new dam intended to block the river and turn

1

Snakeshead Valley into one of the largest lakes in the region.

The victory of the pro-dam faction had been hard won. For the good of the greater land mass Snakeshead Valley had to be sacrificed, but arguments against it had raged for years. There had been three shootings, two deaths since the dam was first proposed, and Bentley thought there might be others before the project was completed. Tempers still ran high in the Crossing, the town that had built up below the damsite around the shallows where the Whitewater could be forded. It lay under the curiously shaped rock that was the last outthrust of the hills on the west, a landmark that old Albert Floyd had insisted looked like the head of a striking rattlesnake.

For himself, Cal Bentley had never seen the resemblance, but Floyd had so named the big valley above it. Floyd had been the original settler and until his son had died under the bullets of one of Boss Herbert's Box H riders he had remained its leading citizen. The boy's death had robbed Floyd of purpose in life, of interest in doing anything. He had become a broken old man and grief had led to whiskey. Alcohol could not make him forget but it did ruin his will and numbed his sharp mind so that he let everything slip away.

First the bank had gone, then the general store, and finally the Snakeshead ranch. Boss Herbert had gobbled that up as he did most that was of value in the Whitewater River country.

Along with Bert Floyd's other friends Cal Bentley had helplessly watched the disintegration of the once big, powerful, commanding figure. Now the old man spent his waking hours huddled in the rear corner of the hotel saloon. He had built the place and still held title to it but he no longer operated it himself. The rent he received paid for his meals, for the second floor room he occupied and for the bottles that he endlessly emptied down his flaccid throat. Still, he never cried. Even when he was so drunk he could barely stand he asked neither help nor pity from anyone.

Cal Bentley shook his head to clear it of the unhappy thoughts and sagged against the corner of the swaying coach. He was tired and depressed rather than enjoying his triumph. The hearings on the dam had been a long, acrimonious wrangle, so ugly that even his winning did not do much to lift his spirits.

The stage dipped down into the curving switchbacks, dropping off the rim for the final run down to the flat and the town on the river. From the window Bentley had a birdseye view of the ragged splotch of the Crossing's lights and knew that in another ten minutes they would pull up before the wooden gallery of the Floyd House.

The only other passenger, sleeping across from Bentley, waked as the coach angle changed. Bentley could make out his bulk as he shifted to look through the window, but could not see the features.

"Much further, friend?"

Cal Bentley did not like being called friend, especially in the slightly patronizing tone in which the man had addressed the native people at the stops. He had used it in the stage station at the Capital, when they had laid over for the noonday meal, had used it speaking to the driver, and now he was using it on Bentley. Cal said shortly.

"A few minutes more."

During daylight Bentley had noted the man's derby hat shoved well back on a head of curly auburn hair, the long mustache and the short, wide coat lapels and tabbed him for a dude. He half smiled, guessing what would happen when the man walked into a Crossing saloon. The boys there could be a little rough on this sort of stranger.

"You from around here?" The man seemed determined to make conversation.

"Yes."

"How big is this Crossing burg?"

"Four thousand, maybe five by now. New people have been coming in the last couple of years."

"Why?"

Bentley did not want to talk to him but he was courteous by nature and training. "We're going to build a dam for a new irrigation district and people are waiting to take up land."

"*Going* to build? When?"

"Engineers are due for the initial surveys next week. They expect completion in about a year."

The man had a mocking bray for a laugh. "Sounds like the farmers are jumping the gun some, I'd say."

Cal Bentley let a little of his irritation into his voice. "They're hoping to catch on with jobs at the dam. It's going to take a lot of horses and scrapers and men to stack up dirt enough to dam the Whitewater. What's your interest in it?"

"Why, I was wondering what kind of market I could expect. I'm in whiskey, you know."

That figured, Bentley thought. The drummer fumbled in his traveling kit and offered a flat bottle.

"Have a sample. Best Pennsylvania mash whiskey money can buy."

Bentley did not really want the drink but he took a sip, corked the bottle and extended it.

"Keep it," the drummer waved it away. "I got a lot more back in the boot and a wagonload coming from Wellford."

"Planning on opening a saloon?"

"Not for me, friend, let the other fellow handle the drunks and dead beats. I take a fair commission and run. How many saloons down there now?"

"Seven, but with the way the town's growing there'll be more soon."

Gratefully Bentley felt the stage swing around the last looping curve and level off into the main street, heard the driver curse the horses into a run until he hauled up with sliding wheels before the hotel. He got down at once, waited for the driver to toss his grip off the top, then walked into the lobby, escaping the drummer who waited for the boot to be opened.

Able Allen was coming down the stairs from the second floor. Cal Bentley stiffened. It was always the same when he saw the banker, they sparked like flint and steel. Allen paused on the lower step and for a long moment they looked at each other in heavy silence, then the banker came down to the lobby floor and stalked past Bentley, saying nothing, and went out to the street.

He had barely gone through the door when Dude Harris came into the lobby from the saloon next door, looking after the retreating banker with an expression of relief. Bentley had an annoyed feeling that his friend had waited deliberately out of sight until Allen had left the building, and wondered why. It was not like Harris to avoid meeting any man. I'm seeing things, he thought. This town has been on edge so long that I expect trouble where there isn't any. Then Harris turned to him and Bentley saw that he was more than a little drunk. Liquor never told in Harris's speech or manner but his eyes took on a brittle glitter.

"Stage late."

It was a chronic complaint not deserving of a comment and Bentley made none. "Who all's in town?"

Dude Harris understood what the question meant. "Boss Herbert, and he brought a lot of troops with him."

"Where?"

Harris jerked his blond head at the saloon door. "Playing blackjack and losing a bundle. I've seen grizzlies with a sore paw in a better humor."

Cal carried his grip around the high desk and set it on the floor under the key rack. The clerk was not in sight, was probably in the kitchen eating his late supper.' As he straightened around, sound on the stairs

6

drew his attention that way. Beth Herbert was halfway down the flight.

The memory of Able Allen coming down those stairs only moments before flashed through him with a wave of jealousy, then he pushed the thought away. The hotel had twenty-four rooms and Beth Herbert might be spending the night in any one of them as she always did when she came in from the ranch.

Still, the knowledge that she and Allen had been upstairs, perhaps together, sickened him. He could never make up his mind about her thinking. They had grown up together, through grade school and high school. He had courted her but when the time came for him to go east to college she would not give him an answer. When he returned his whole world here was changed. Beth's father had taken Snakeshead ranch away from Albert Floyd and was now the district's dominant citizen. Able Allen, a newcomer, had bought out the crumbled remains of the bank and was determinedly drawing together the strings of other businesses in his supple fingers. And apparently he had also taken in Beth Herbert and Cal Bentley was rejected.

Shapely, fair and poised the girl came down to a step that put their eyes on a level and stopped, unsmiling, glanced at Dude Harris and said peremptorily,

"Go on, Dude, I want to talk to Cal alone."

Dude grunted, lifted an offended shoulder and went back to the saloon. Cal told her in a low, even tone,

"That wasn't very wise, Beth."

7

She was a tall girl, five feet ten, made to look taller by the high heeled riding boots. She showed him a quick annoyance.

"Why should I care what Dude thinks?"

"He likes to talk."

"Let him gossip. Let the town think whatever it likes, they used to link us together often enough. I don't care."

This was not the way she used to be. She had been laughter and fun and an easy companion, and he winced at her unfeeling voice now, saying more sharply than he intended,

"I do care."

Her lips bent down, mocking. "Does the great victorious attorney fear his reputation might be tarnished?"

He smarted, then rallied and grinned at her. "You are right, an officer of the court should never fall under suspicion."

"Very funny. All I want is to warn you that my father has a dozen of the crew in town and in his present mood you'll do well to keep away from him."

Cal Bentley stopped smiling and his eyes hardened, his voice roughened. "Beth, I won't avoid any man, your father or anyone else. I have to talk to him and if he chooses to take a personal affront because he was beaten in a law suit . . ."

"Ruined in a law suit, if you have your way."

"He could have accepted the government's offer for the ranch buildings. He was just too bullheaded and greedy."

Her mouth dropped open. The idea that anyone would say such a thing about Boss Herbert left her gasping. Cal Bentley did not give her time to explode, but turned away and walked through the door into the saloon.

CHAPTER
TWO

The saloon was big, noisy, overhung by a curtain of blue tobacco smoke that screened the dingy ceiling. A quick glance showed Bentley a lineup of men along the whole of the bar and he recognized many of them as Herbert's crew. As he crossed the room he saw that their eyes followed him in the backbar mirror, like panthers watching a lone sheep. In spite of his tight control the short hairs at the back of his neck crawled. But he did not pause.

Albert Floyd sat at his rear table with a full bottle of whiskey at his elbow, his claw thin hand around a glass, his old eyes glassy and staring, fixed on nothing in this world, perhaps on the memory of dreams of long before.

Two poker tables and the blackjack layout were running. Blackjack was not a common game in the territory but Foster North, who ran the saloon on lease from Floyd, had started his career in St. Louis as a blackjack dealer and it pleased him to continue dealing the game whenever he could find a customer.

Tonight four men faced him across the kidney shaped table. Boss Herbert on the near end, looking bulky in the town clothes . . . Dewey Styles who kept the livery, Lenard who owned the feed store, and at the far end Joe Garvey, Herbert's foreman.

Even if Dude Harris had not forewarned Bentley that Herbert was losing heavily Cal would have guessed it from the scowl on the rancher's big face as he studied his cards. Bentley reached the table and stopped at the side to watch the hand out.

Herbert scuffed the card hidden in his thick hand toward him and said in a tight voice, "Hit me."

North dealt him a deuce, face up. Herbert swore.

"Damn it. Hit me again."

North dealt him a trey. Herbert growled, debating with himself. North had a king showing and what he had in the hole was the mystery. Herbert made up his mind.

"Hit me again."

He caught a queen and flipped the cards away in disgust. "That busts it."

North did not change expression as he raked in the bet. Bentley was surprised to see Herbert playing twenty-dollar gold pieces because gambling at the Crossing was usually held to fairly small stakes. The rancher sat slumped in his chair, hesitating over whether to quit and take his losses or try again. He turned his head to motion a bartender for a fresh bottle and saw Bentley. Abruptly he squared half around, thrust out his lower jaw and grated,

"What the hell you gawking at?"

Cal kept his voice level. Once he had expected that this burly man would be his father-in-law. "I am waiting until you are free. I want to talk to you."

"Talk."

"In private."

"I got nothing to say to you private."

Bentley's voice continued flat, without emotion. "As you choose. Colonel Ruggles sends you word that he wants your fences down and the cows out of Snakeshead Valley in accordance with the court order. The first survey crews will be in here next week and they have orders to shoot any cattle that get in their way."

Boss Herbert appeared to swell like a giant toad. He started out of his chair but Joe Garvey was faster, spinning up and planting his rawhide-tough body between his employer and Cal Bentley.

"Let me have the bastard." The voice was low, the face wolfish. "I been looking forward to this a long, long time."

Herbert said nothing and Garvey took it as permission and in that moment he threw an overhand blow, charging in. Garvey had earned a reputation as a barroom fighter, had crippled Hans Frederick so the German would never walk again, but Cal had boxed during his college years.

He sidestepped, ducked under the flaying arm and felt the sweep of the roundhouse as it brushed his shoulder. Before Garvey recovered Bentley hit him in the mouth, pulping the drawn lips between his fist and the hard teeth. Garvey backed away spitting out blood and two front teeth, lowered his head and butted.

Bentley tried to sidestep again but bumped into Foster North who was trying to wrestle his precious

12

blackjack table out of the way of the fight, and pinned there Cal could not dodge the foreman's swinging fists, one to the side of his head, one over his heart. Bentley went down, carrying the table as it broke, carrying North with him to the floor.

Garvey came in to kick at his side but North's shoulder took the brunt of the boot while Bentley flung loose from the wreckage and got drunkenly to his feet. With an animal's instinct Garvey sensed that Cal was hurt and began to stalk him, but he was over-confident. The red mist that clouded Bentley's eyes cleared and he saw Garvey's savage, triumphant face inches from his own. With the strength of desperation he stepped inside and drove his right with all his strength behind it against Garvey's jaw. Garvey's head cracked back, his eyes crossed and he fell, his head cracking against a table leg with a popping sound.

Cal Bentley stood swaying, looking down on the foreman, and when Garvey did not move to get up he wiped blood from his bruised face and turned away. Boss Herbert's voice clubbed at him from behind.

"Stop right where you are, this isn't over yet. It's just begun."

Bentley looked across at the bar, at the riders there watching him like leashed lions ready to spring. Herbert's voice went higher.

"We're going to teach you a lesson, lawyer boy, then we're going to tar and feather you and start you across the hills on a mule, riding backward."

The line of men straightened, starting to prowl forward. Bentley wore a gun at his hip and had used it since his boyhood, but to draw it was exactly what they wanted him to do, give them an excuse to shoot him down. Herbert now was enjoying himself as a natural bully, wanting to force Bentley to crawl, to beg for mercy.

"Rowley, you and Haynes hold his arms. I want to see how many punches he can take."

He stood up and made a ritual of rolling his right sleeve to the elbow. Bentley didn't look back to see him but watched the two riders come away from the bar and quarter toward him, measuring them, trying to think of a way out. Just before they came within reach Dude Harris's lazy drawl cut down the length of the room.

"Look over this way, boys, then stand pat."

All heads turned toward the bandy legged man leaning against the wall near Albert Floyd's table and the guns in each of his rather small hands. Boss Herbert had swung on a boot heel and rage made a crimson devil mask of his face. He roared across the space.

"Dude, you put those things away and clear out of here."

"Not likely."

"I won't forget this . . ."

"Why," Dude said, "I don't know that I'd want you to." His voice hardened. "The lot of you move over and face the south wall. When I give the word the guy at the west end pulls his gun, slow, and drops it, then the next guy and the next. Somebody got a cute idea, forget it. I don't miss. Get going."

14

They went sullenly, hate filling the room like a flow of molten rock. The only two who did not feel it were Joe Garvey, still unconscious, and Albert Floyd in his alcoholic stupor. One by one the men let their guns fall, thudding dully on the splintered floor, then at Dude's next order they backed to the bar.

"Cal," Dude said, "gather up the hardware."

Bentley called to the bartenders. "Get me a sack."

One of them pulled a flour sack that was used as a bar towel from under the counter. Bentley took it to where the guns lay and dropped them in, straightened and faced the bar.

"I'll leave this at the livery. Don't hurry to get there."

Boss Herbert cursed him in a choked voice, shaking his fist, then shouted. "That dam is never going to be built, Bentley, make up your mind to that."

Bentley said coldly, "The government says different."

"To hell with the government. You and your Colonel Ruggles figure you've got everything locked up but you're going to learn you don't. We've got a few angles of our own."

Cal Bentley did not argue the matter. In a way he couldn't blame the rancher. When you had been using half a million government acres to run your cows on, it came as a shock to know it is going to be taken away.

Boss Herbert had made a private preserve of the Snakeshead Valley, by sheer gall and ruthlessness driving the smaller ranchers out of it and into the foothills. Then he had strung fences up both sides of the valley, in effect creating a pasture of nearly five-hundred-thousand acres with the river running through it.

But when the dam was built the whole of Snakeshead would be under water and the graze Herbert had enjoyed for so long would be drowned. Where could he move his animals? Up the side canyons and onto the higher hills? Those canyons were already filled with the men he had run out of the valley, and added to these were the hundreds of people who had been pouring in since the first announcement that a dam was planned.

The latter were for the most part not cattlemen, they had come out of the east, farmers, small town residents who were squeezed out of their homes by the depression that gripped that part of the country. They made a sorry sight with their goods and families loaded aboard creaking wagons under canvas-covered bows, their stock herded behind by half-grown boys and at times girls. The message of the new irrigation district to be created had apparently floated on the wind and they were gathering, forming a town of their own across the Whitewater from the Crossing, a town of huts and shacks built with parts of their sun-dried wagons. Others were living like gophers in holes dug into the rocky hillsides and roofed with sod.

Cal Bentley had watched the influx with his own sense of foreboding, picturing the emigrants' mounting problems when the blazing summer sun gave way to the bitter blizzards that racked this country in the winter months. They were too many, coming too soon, for construction jobs on the dam were still months away,

16

and they could not take up land around the lake-shore until the surveys were completed.

Now he left the saloon with Dude Harris and walked toward the livery, tramped into the runway and while Dude got their horses Cal Bentley took the sack of guns into the barn office and dumped it on the scarred desk. They saddled quickly and swung up, but even so the Herbert riders were running out of the saloon as they rode off toward the river. They forded at the shallows and turned north along the far bank through the shack town. Almost at once they came into the hills that bordered a side valley and took the trail, climbing steadily.

Dude Harris broke the silence only then. "I don't get it, Cal."

"Don't get what?"

"What Boss Herbert thinks he's about. He has a lot of riders but he can't buck the government."

Cal Bentley had been considering the same question. Boss was stubborn but he was not stupid and he must have some idea up his sleeve or he would not dare disobey the court order that directed him to remove his fences, his barns and cattle from Snakeshead Valley.

"We'll find out sooner or later," he said. "Ruggles will be here with his crews to survey."

"What about Brandy? Isn't it up to him to see the order is obeyed?"

Bentley pulled up his horse and looked at Harris in embarrassment. "You do have something there. I should have talked to him when I first got in but that business with Herbert made me forget. I'll do it now."

He turned the horse back and Dude started to turn but Bentley told him, "You ride on home, I won't be caught off base a second time."

The older rider did not like Bentley returning to town alone but he did not argue. Cal had a stubborn streak of his own and he would not change his mind once he had spoken. Harris watched until the darkness swallowed the other man and horse, then took up the trail again.

Sheriff Brandy Ives's small grey home behind the courthouse was dark, his night patrolling finished. Not wanting a second run in with Boss Herbert, Cal Bentley came by the back street, rode around to the rear and tied his horse, then rapped on the kitchen door. He knocked four times before he heard movement inside. A match flared and lamplight glowed up, then the bolt on the door was drawn and Ives opened it in his nightshirt, holding the lamp over his head. His eyes were not yet adjusted to the light and he said sleepily,

"Who is it?"

"Cal Bentley, Brandy . . ."

Brandy Ives sounded accusing. "What you want this time of night, knocking a God-fearing man out of his just sleep?"

"Save it for Sunday meeting," Bentley said. "I'm coming in for five minutes so back out of the way."

The sheriff was a tall, thin man past middle age and the legs below the hem of the nightshirt showed very little muscle over the bones. He retreated reluctantly. They had never been close but Brandy was too much the politician to want a quarrel with anyone, certainly not the Crossing's young leading attorney.

"Didn't know you was back." Ives set the lamp on the kitchen table. "Drink?"

"Thanks."

Ives brought a bottle and two water glasses and seemed nervous as he poured, clinking the neck of the bottle on the rims of the glasses. He handed one drink to Bentley, said, "Cheers," and drank his liquor in one swallow.

Cal sipped. "Got in this evening but it's been a little busy. I wanted to tell you Ruggles and his surveyors will be here next week and the orders are for Herbert to be out of Snakeshead by then."

Brandy's pale tongue ran around his flat lips. "That's kind of rough, Cal."

"How? He's known for six months what the court decided."

"The lower court."

"So he appealed, but even his own lawyers warned him he couldn't win a reversal."

Brandy sounded aggrieved. "You don't have to get huffy with me . . . You better tell Herbert."

"I just did." Bentley felt of his bruised jaw and Ives, seeing it, smiled crookedly.

"I judge he didn't take too kindly to the news."

"He as much as told me he intends to ignore the order to vacate. Now it's up to you to implement the order."

Brandy Ives shook his shaggy head in a slow cadence and poured himself a second drink. "Huh-uh, Cal, no it ain't. I'm not sheriff any more. I resigned."

For a moment Cal Bentley did not believe the man. Brandy had held the post for better than ten years and loved it. He loved parading the street with the star polished on his open vest, loved visiting the restaurants for a free cup of coffee and stopping in the saloons for a complimentary whiskey. Then Bentley understood that Ives' fear of offending Boss Herbert was greater than his love of the job. He said,

"Who is acting sheriff?"

"Nobody. My deputies quit with me. The commissioners met but they couldn't find a single man would take the place. I'm right sorry, Cal."

He did not sound sorry. He sounded highly amused.

CHAPTER
THREE

Bentley's home ranch, the place where he had been brought up and still maintained, ran up from the mouth of a small side canyon with a stream tumbling through it toward the main river a mile below Cal's boundary. It had been his father's, a lawyer before Cal who preferred living in the isolated privacy to a clapboard house in the Crossing where petitioners could get at him too easily to beg free legal advice.

In a land where ranches were counted in fifty-thousand-acre blocks his five hundred acres were a laughing stock as a place to run a herd, and he would not have bothered with the two hundred cows he did keep except that he wanted to give Dude Harris something to do.

Harris had managed the little spread for the elder Bentley since before Cal was born, had taught the boy to ride and shoot and play cards and been his friend. Without knowing just how old the rider was Cal judged he was in his sixties. He knew little about Dude's history behind his own memory. Dude was a notorious gossip but it never included anything about himself, and the one time he had asked his father when he was very young the attorney had lectured him. One thing you never did in this country was ask a man about his past.

"Anything he did or was before he came here is his affair, not yours. It's the way he acts here and now that counts."

Cal did learn one bit of information from One Lung, which was not the Oriental's real name. That was old Amos Bentley's joke and the old Chinese who had cooked for them as long as Cal could remember would have answered to anything his idol chose to call him. They had met one day when Bentley had found the Chinese treed by a railroad-town mob that wanted the sport of hanging him by his queue, had held them off with his guns and told the frightened Oriental to climb down and get up behind his saddle. When they had raced away the mob made no attempt to follow, content to drink up the Chinaman's money that they had found under his mattress.

One Lung had been desolated because the money was being saved to send his body back to China for a proper funeral. He had not yet needed the funeral and Cal suspected that by now he had enough accumulated for several such celebrations when his time came.

One Lung had told Cal an incident about Dude Harris because of the similarity with his own rescue. Amos had picked up Harris from a lynch party and taken him with them when he came north to settle in the Snakeshead area, but Cal never learned why Harris was to be hanged.

It was three hours after midnight when he finally rode into his yard, but every lamp was burning and

Harris came from the kitchen door at his hail and took the horse. Cal crossed the yard bone tired and feeling every punch he had taken in the saloon fight. Inside the kitchen One Lung had heard the hail and was at the big stove dishing up smoking meat and beans and pan biscuits. Bentley settled at the table and sank against the chair back. The Chinese brought strong, hot coffee laced with whiskey and some of the tiredness ran out of Cal before the black liquid.

That and the food smell brought up a ravenous hunger. He had not eaten since the noon stage stop and the meal had been too poor to stomach much of. The plate was already nearly empty when Dude Harris pulled open the screen door and came in, moving with a young man's balanced grace in spite of his years. He poured coffee for himself and sat down across from Bentley.

"How'd you make out with Brandy?"

Cal Bentley shook his head.

"What do you mean? He won't support a court order?"

"He's resigned as sheriff." Bentley's voice was a weary sigh.

Harris set his cup carefully on the table. "Brandy Ives?"

"He's scared of Boss Herbert."

"Oh. Yeah. That figures. Who's sheriff now?"

"Nobody. The commissioners can't find anyone to serve. Or that's what Brandy claims."

Harris picked up the cup and studied the inside as if there were something to learn there. "What happens now?"

"I'll talk to them tomorrow and if they won't act I'll appeal to the government to send in federal marshals . . . What's new around here?"

Dude's voice was carefully neutral. "You've got visitors."

Bentley looked at him, not liking the sound of it, and waited. Harris went on in the same tone.

"Several wagons in the upper end of the canyon. They been there awhile but I just saw their fires when I came up tonight. I rode on for a look-see and warned them not to come down past the fork. They're some uppity, told me to go to hell, said this is government property and they'd damn well light where they had a mind to."

Bentley finished his supper before he said anything more, then he shoved back. "I've had enough for today, I'll see them in the morning."

He climbed heavily to his room and was asleep as soon as he hit the bed, and the sun was full up over the eastern rim before he stirred.

Carrying a towel, he walked naked down the south meadow to the edge of the hustling stream and into it. The chill water tightened and brought life to his stiff muscles but every spot Joe Garvey's hard fists had caught him ached individually. He rubbed himself down in the warm sun, then went back to the house and One Lung's steak and cakes.

He and Dude ate in silence and in silence they went to the corral, saddled horses and swung up, taking the trail that led upcanyon through the scatter of grazing cattle. The bowl above was perhaps, a mile across,

24

nestled between the high rims that rose like a bulwark on three sides. On the fourth, the little stream had over many years cut a break through the rising rock. Through it Cal Bentley had an astonishing view.

He rode through, looking around him. Two weeks ago there had been no one in this bowl. Now seven cabins had been built of logs cut from the trees on the slopes. Several soddies were burrowed into the steep banks. Children played between the houses, chickens scratched in the tall grass talking comfortably among themselves and women were washing along the stream, pounding clothes on the rocks for want of soap. A tall man detached himself from a building team and stalked forward to meet Bentley and Harris. There was no welcome in his manner or his gaunt face and his voice was curt.

"Riding for fun or you want something?"

Bentley eased his knee over the saddle horn and began rolling a cigarette, saying quietly.

"You're on my ground."

"No we ain't. This is government land and open to anyone."

"Not here."

They measured each other, the man's jaw thrust out. "That's what they told me."

"Who?"

"In the new town this side from the Crossing."

"They told you wrong."

The man's voice went up, belligerent. "They say they checked in the land office in the Territorial Capital and all the land in Snakeshead Valley is open."

Bentley kept his tone quiet. "This is not Snakeshead Valley. My father homesteaded here the year I was born."

"I don't believe you."

The new voice caught them unaware, a light, female voice, and Bentley and Harris turned to look behind them. A towheaded girl stood braced there with a rifle trained on Bentley's chest. He spoke mildly.

"You'd better put that down before somebody gets hurt, Miss."

"If anyone does it will be you, Mister." She used her left hand to brush a strand of hair away from her eye but the rifle barrel did not quiver an inch. "I can shoot the eye out of a squirrel at a hundred yards."

Bentley's lips twitched. "You couldn't see a squirrel's eye at a hundred yards. Lower the gun, you can't prove anything with it."

Her legs were apart and she squirmed the heels deeper. "We're here. Suppose you try to move us out."

Cal Bentley had a sudden uncontrollable surge of laughter. It was not only the slight, young figure threatening. The joke was on him. Who would he call on to move them anywhere? There wasn't any sheriff and the county commissioners weren't looking for one. He glanced at Dude who was not laughing.

"Come on, this can wait."

"Leave your guns." It was the girl's tight voice.

Bentley kept smiling. The tone told him she probably would shoot, and she was too close to miss, too far away to stop. Further, the team working on the cabin had stopped and picked up their rifles. There was nothing to be gained by argument and at the odds these people were not going to be impressed by threats. He nodded easily, pulled his forty-five, careful not to make a move they could misinterpret, and let it slide to the thick grass carpet, drew his rifle from the boot and dropped it, then his eyes told Harris to do the same.

He saw the rage inside the rider and for a moment was afraid Dude might be foolish enough to make a try, and said sharply,

"No."

The moment drew out, then Harris grudgingly dropped his guns, yanked his horse around and drove away. As Bentley swung his animal to follow the girl's high call hit at his back.

"Don't you either one come back. Never. The first time we see you we shoot."

Below the bowl Dude hauled up and sat waiting until Bentley caught him. He was still boiling.

"What the hell's the world coming to? Herbert can buffalo Brandy into quitting and now these damn farmers calmly camp on your ranch and set up like they expect to stay . . ."

Bentley kept his voice quiet. "I've an idea they intend to."

"What are we going to do about it?"

Bentley shrugged. He was not really too concerned about the squatters. He was not using the bowl as pasture at the time and once the trouble with Boss Herbert was settled and law was again functioning it would be a simple matter to go into court, prove the land was his and have them put off.

"You got any suggestions? From the number of wagons I'd say there must be anyhow twenty men. You think the two of us could handle them?"

"No, nor that crazy girl. She's got no right to act like that . . . taking advantage that she's a woman and a man can't rightly throw down on one." Dude sounded bitterly incensed.

"Then let's forget it for now. I have to ride in and talk to the commissioners."

"We'd better stop by home for some guns on the way."

Bentley thought that over and decided against the idea. "I don't think so, Dude. We don't need them at the Crossing unless the Box H is still in town, and this time of year Herbert can't keep the crew away from ranch work too much."

Harris grumbled but he turned his horse in beside Bentley's and they crossed the stream to put the animals up the canyonside to the deer trail short cut that saved more than ten miles of riding. It was coming on noon when they passed through the shack town, forded the Whitewater and so came into the main street of the Crossing.

The town looked empty with blinds half drawn at the store windows against the overhead sun, and only an occasional figure moved down the slatted sidewalk. They stopped in the courthouse yard and left the horses in the shade of the big cottonwood and walked to the hotel. There would be no one in the courthouse at this hour and those who did not go home to eat would be in the hotel dining room.

Bentley was lucky. Three of the five county commissioners were gathered at the long table and he sat down opposite them. The waitress brought food and mugs of coffee, serving American plan. You took what was put before you, there was no choice. Two of the commissioners were men he had known since his childhood, Moses Foster, the butcher, and Morton Thompson from the barbershop. The third was the banker, Able Allen, from whom Cal could expect no help. Allen looked up quickly as Bentley sat down, then dropped his eyes and concentrated on his plate. Bentley nodded to the others.

"I understand we haven't got a sheriff?"

Thompson was a little man with a small face dwarfed by bushy sideburns that worked as if they had a life of their own when he chewed or talked. He chewed now and said nothing. Moses Foster was thick, his arms big and powerful from handling his carcasses. He swallowed and said,

"That's right."

"When are you going to appoint one?"

"When we find him."

"Meaning?"

Foster took a measured time to answer and an edge of anger came into his voice. "You know the situation, Cal. You should . . . You're responsible for it."

Cal Bentley used his cool legal tone. "No, Moses, the court is. I only represented the water company. It's Herbert's own fault that he didn't file on any of that land when he took over the ranch. I know why he didn't and I can't sympathize . . . He figured that if he filed on the quarter section where his buildings are other men would commence filing in the Valley. So long as he could scare them out he had the place sewed up, but he made a serious mistake. Colonel Ruggles pulled enough weight in Washington to get the Valley designated an irrigation district and the dam is going in no matter what Boss Herbert or you people think.

"Moses . . . Morton . . . not appointing a sheriff is not going to alter that fact. It may delay the work temporarily, but if it's necessary Ruggles will bring in enough federal marshals to physically throw Herbert and his crew out. So you had better appoint someone now."

"No." Able Allen pounded the handle of his knife on the table, once.

Bentley's mouth thinned and tightened. "I should think you would be the first to want a sheriff. If the outlaws up in the high hills hear the county is unprotected they'll ride down here and scoop up whatever it is you keep in the bank safe."

"I've thought of that." Allen touched his napkin to his mouth, then gave Bentley a wintry smile. "I have set it up with Herbert to loan me a couple of his men as private guards until this fight is finished."

"When do you expect that to be?"

"When the Supreme Court rules against the water people."

Bentley spoke to the little barber. "Are you content with that arrangement?"

30

The pale hands fluttered and the man sounded nervous. "Not entirely, Cal . . . but what choice have we? Where do we find anybody who isn't afraid to go up against Herbert?"

Bentley had been thinking about that all during the ride to town and he had found only one possible solution.

"I'm not. Appoint me."

Allen's fork stopped in mid-air, then he continued raising it slowly. The other two looked at Bentley with open mouths.

"Appoint . . ." the butcher gasped, "But . . ."

Bentley's voice turned hard. "Don't you think I am qualified?"

"Well, sure . . . but, but but . . ."

Cal concentrated on Foster and Thompson as the more likely to be frightened into caving. "Listen to me. The small ranchers Herbert drove out do not agree with you and neither do all the people in town or around the county. Furthermore all these new people coming in are against Herbert. They want the dam and they can all vote. I am going to call a meeting, and if you refuse to act I'll call for a special election. I wonder how many of the present commissioners will be reelected."

The butcher and barber looked startled, then worried. Moses Foster cleared his throat loudly but his words were still choked.

"Well . . . give me an hour to talk to the other boys . . ."

"I'll be in the bar."

Able Allen glared, shoved his chair back noisily and got up. That, Bentley knew, was one vote he had no chance of winning.

CHAPTER
FOUR

The new sheriff of Snakeshead County stood across the desk from his lone deputy. The desk was more battered, scarred and splintered than the one in the office Cal Bentley had inherited from his father, although there were many marks of boots and spurs on the top of that one too. Dude Harris scratched at his thatch of grey-peppered blond hair and gave Bentley his wry grin, his eyes on the polished star Bentley had just pinned on his shirt.

"Never thought I'd see the day when I'd play at being a law man. If my old pappy could see me now he'd roll right up out of his grave. He never had much use for law . . . it interfered with his drinking time."

"Don't let it go to your head." Bentley laughed at him. "The first thing we need is a lot more deputies . . . twenty or thirty before we'll be able to take Boss Herbert out of that valley . . ."

"Sure . . . sure . . . where do you think you'll dig up anybody else at all to ride with you?"

"I've been thinking about the new people across the river."

"Farmers? Hell . . . You expect that kind to stand up to Herbert's crew of toughs? Think again, Cal."

Bentley made the comparison and admitted to himself that Harris was probably right, that Eastern farmers were not trained for the kind of fight that would be coming. He walked thoughtfully to the open front window that let the rising heat of the new day begin to turn the office into a furnace. His eye caught riders up the street and when he looked squarely toward them Boss Herbert was at the head of a column of his men, just splashing across the ford. It was too soon for a confrontation. He swung to Harris.

"Out the back way, now, or our term of office is going to be the shortest in history."

They snatched rifles and short guns out of the glass front case against the wall and ran down the passage toward the rear entrance of the courthouse, yanking the door open. There they stopped. Able Allen stood outside, a gun in his hands leveled on them. His voice held a chilly pleasure.

"Come on out, you two."

They stepped through the door slowly.

"Drop the rifles and turn around, face the building and lean forward against your hands."

There was nothing else to do except get shot. They stood, off balance, while Allen took the short guns and stepped away, saying,

"Go back to the office and sit down, you're going to have visitors."

Allen trailed them through the empty corridor. Bentley took the chair behind the desk, Harris one at the corner of it. They heard the horses arrive outside and the jangle of spurs as the riders stepped down, then

34

the front door was kicked open and Boss Herbert came through with Joe Garvey close behind, his face still marked by Bentley's fists. Both had guns in their hands. Seven men came after them and lined against the wall, hungry grins on all of them. Able Allen chuckled, a rasping sound.

"Our new sheriff is unsociable. He and Dude were just leaving."

Herbert faced Bentley and spoke in a tone of mock grief as if a friend he counted on had let him down. "Cal, I thought you had better sense than to try a stupid stunt like this."

Bentley watched him and said nothing. The rancher went on.

"You were more talkative last night . . . But get it out of your head that you're going to keep that badge. Take it off and give it to me."

Cal Bentley did not speak, did not move. The big rancher shouted in sudden fury.

"Stand up, you."

Cal got to his feet, taking his time. Herbert stumped to the side of the desk and threw a hard blow into Bentley's face, knocking the lawyer back over the chair to fall in a tangle with it. He was not out but he was dazed, not aware that Dude Harris with an animal growl put one hand on the desk, sprang to the top and launched himself onto Herbert's back. The rider clung around him like a spider and his old hands tore at Herbert's throat.

Three of Herbert's men clawed him off, beat him over the head with gun barrels. Harris went to the floor and they still clubbed him, then Joe Garvey and Rowley grabbed Bentley's arms and hauled him to his feet, holding him.

Boss Herbert spat in Cal's face. "Take him out and tie him on his horse. Fetch Dude along." His hand snaked out to the star and tore it off Bentley's shirt, ripping the cloth.

They marched Bentley staggering out to the street. The heat hit him, made his aching head dizzy. They hoisted him into his saddle, tied his wrists to the high horn and his ankles with a rope under the animal's belly, and there was no way he could resist. He slumped, sick and aching, with last night's battering reawakened by the new attack. He saw Dude Harris dragged, limp, out of the courthouse and dumped across his horse and for one long anguished moment feared the Dude was dead, then the rider groaned and tried to thrash right side up in the saddle, failed and fell back. Fury gave Bentley the strength to shout.

"Damn it, straighten him up before all the blood runs to his head."

Herbert's heavy laugh came. "Head's empty anyhow, won't hurt to fill it with something." He walked to the horse and yanked Dude's head up by the hair until their faces were close together. "I told you the other night I wouldn't forget your butting in. Garvey, you and Rowley sit him up and rope him on so he stays put. It's easier on the horse."

Bentley watched as Dude was put astride and roped, bent forward against the horn and tied to it to keep him from falling off. Then the crew mounted and Boss

36

Herbert led the parade down the main street and out of town. People watched from store doorways, from saloons and the hotel porch. Not one moved to stop the line.

Bitterly Cal Bentley saw how fear of the power of one man could immobilize an entire town. It took leadership to make five thousand people rise against this bully and no one was willing to step forward, to risk his neck. Even when they forded the river and passed between the scattered wagons and shacks the men stared briefly and turned away. Did they not know what was in store for them if Herbert was not challenged and beaten? One of his next moves would be to drive them out of the country. They were a danger to him, for when the families ran out of money and got hungry the vast herd of Box H cattle would be too tempting to resist.

They rode. The hurt in his head made his mind waver between awareness and vagueness. He lost track of time. They were heading west. Occasionally he wondered why Herbert should take them so far. They passed a stand of aspen, trees plenty tall enough to swing a man's feet off the ground. And still they continued.

A growing suspicion began to come through to him. The character of the land was changing. They crossed a ridge and then another and finally dropped down into a badlands of broken lava, sand and rock that could not support even a cactus.

The Burning Land. That was what the Indians had called it. They had said the spirit of evil lived in the weathered, blistering breaks of the shattered old volcanic spill and they avoided it like a plague.

In a flash of illumination Bentley knew what Herbert meant to do. He had brought them out here to set them afoot, leave them to die.

There was no water within twenty miles. It was doubtful if a strong and healthy man could make it back to the river and a certainty that he and Dude, with the beatings they had undergone, could never walk there.

They crossed an area of tumbled lava boulders with parched sand between and came to a twisting gorge twenty feet deep where the caprock had split as it cooled. There Boss Herbert held up a hand, reined around and rode to Bentley's side.

"This ought to be far enough. You think so, Bentley?"

Cal looked at him through a red haze of pain. "Boss, for Christ sake shoot us or hang us."

Herbert grinned, pleased with himself and wanting to brag. "You should have looked ahead to what you was getting into a way back. It just don't occur to you smart-ass bastards that a man with the will don't have to knuckle under to your rules. You're so cock sure the law man will be around to get you off the hook that you go bulling in where you don't belong. Now you don't really think I'm stupid enough to leave you around hanging by a rope or with bullets in you, do you? I'll see your bodies are found before it's too late to tell how you died. There won't be a mark on you . . . oh . . . the ones you already got won't show, but there won't be any stretched necks or knife cuts. You'll just dry up from thirst."

Bentley heard his voice as a croak. He hated to beg, especially of Boss Herbert, but the thought of dying without water in this scorched waste drove him to try.

"At least take Dude back. He's hurt bad. He can't stand much more." Even as the words forced out he cursed himself for giving Herbert the opening to gloat.

Herbert laughed in his face, then raised his voice to the crew. "Get them down and let's clear out. Sun's getting hot."

The men dropped out of the saddles and unbound Dude first, barely catching him as he slid off the horse and lowering him ungently to the ground. The only sign of life in him was a weak groan. Then they were at Bentley's ropes and when those were off they pushed him. He fell heavily on the sharp flint-hard black lava. They gathered in his and Dude's animals, remounted and rode away, back toward the valley.

With the breath jarred out of him Cal Bentley lay still a long while. Finally he had enough air to stir and sit up. His skin was burning with sun and heat, his shoulder ached where he had landed on it. His head pounded and when he put up his hands to hold it the hair was matted with dried blood and grit. He rolled to his hands and knees and stayed there, afraid of the effort of trying to stand. When his trembling lessened enough he crawled to Dude and lowered his head to the chest, listening for heartbeat. Dude was alive. Bentley rocked back on his heels. Startling him, Dude opened his eyes and looked blearily at Bentley.

"Where are we?" The voice was a husky whisper.

"The Burning Land."

Dude's eyes fluttered closed as if he could shut away the thought. "I was afraid of that. They leave us here to die?"

Cal Bentley laid a gentle hand on the old rider's shoulder. "I'm sorry, Dude. I shouldn't have got you into this."

"Hell." The word had surprising strength. "I always kind of wanted to know what it felt like to be a law man. Now I know. You hurt too bad to walk?"

"No. You?"

Dude Harris turned on his stomach, raised himself on his hands, got a grip on a boulder and tried to rise. The cords in his arm stood out with the effort and he got up to one knee, one foot, shoved to stand, then fell.

"Damn it, my knees are jelly. Cal, you go on."

Bentley said, "Go where?"

"Back to the water. You ain't giving up, are you?"

Bentley said nothing but he thought he might as well. There was no use kidding himself that he could reach the river even if he would abandon Dude Harris, and he would not do that.

A sound nicked at him. Or was it imagination? Something like the clink of iron on rock, perhaps a horseshoe. It came again and he was sure. It could be that Boss Herbert had changed his mind, not softened, but worried that they might possibly escape and sent a rider back to watch them until they were dead.

He twisted on his knees. A pale-haired girl was riding around the rock burst they had passed in coming out

40

here. She rode steadily toward them. The towhead who had laid a rifle on them that morning in the bowl . . . and that was a long way away.

The rifle was across her knees and her head turned from side to side, watchful.

Bentley tried to call, to ask for help. He and Dude were down in the cluster of boulders and only the top of his head rose above them. His voice came out a dry croaking that he thought she could not hear. In desperation he fought to his feet, started walking toward her. His boot toe caught on a stone and he pitched down, hard.

His strength spent, he lay, half conscious. Then the clinking started again and grew louder. She was coming his way.

CHAPTER
FIVE

The first thing he was really conscious of was wetness. Water touching his dry and cracking lips. He opened his eyes. It took a great deal of effort to raise the heavy lids. He looked up into her face. She was concentrating on a handkerchief, soaking it from a canteen and squeezing it, dripping it onto his mouth without touching the blistered skin.

"Open your mouth," she said. "Try to swallow. Do you know what I'm saying?"

He tried. Parting his lips was painful, as if it tore the corners of his mouth, and when he swallowed the throat muscles were as stiff as if he had been throttled by powerful hands. She squeezed the cloth again and a little trickle tickled down his parched throat, warm from the canteen, almost hot. He could not remember anything that had ever tasted so good. He stirred to sit up.

She said, "Rest some more."

He moved his head to the side and kept trying, got his back raised and looked toward Harris. Dude lay on his side, his eyes open, watching Bentley and the girl.

"How is he?" Dude's voice was a dry grating.

She looked toward him. "I got a little water in him. He'll come around."

"Hell." Bentley could not decide whether Dude was swearing or trying to describe the land around them.

"What's that?"

"I'll send them to hell."

So hell was the last word of what Dude wanted to say, and Bentley had no doubt who the rider was thinking about. Dude appeared in better condition than he had dared hope. The old cowman was rawhide and iron.

Bentley put a hand out toward the canteen and after a moment's hesitation the girl gave it to him, warning.

"Not too much at a time."

He drank sparingly, returned the can. She took it to Dude, helped him to sit up and drink, moved between them until both men had enough liquid to keep them alive without making them sick, then she walked to the horse tied to a lava upthrust and hung the canteen on the saddle horn, returning to crouch at Bentley's side.

"Are you feeling any stronger?"

His head was clearing more quickly. He nodded, looking toward the sun, seeing how low it was above the western hills.

"Yes. Thank you. You know you saved our lives . . ."

"Uh-huh."

His vocal cords, were working more easily. "I find it embarrassing, after I ordered you out of the bowl yesterday . . ." Had it been only yesterday? It seemed much longer since he had come home, so much had happened.

"About that," she said, "were you telling the truth? You do own the canyon?"

"All of it, yes. But don't let it bother you. I don't need the upper end. I'll deed it to you."

Her eyes widened enormously. They were amber, complementing the warm brown of her sun-tanned face. She stammered in disbelief.

"You . . . you mean you would give it to us?"

"Lady, after what you've done for us I'd give you the whole ranch and anything else I could lay my hands on . . . How did you happen to find us so far from there?"

"I didn't happen to. I followed you. I was down at the river in the shack town visiting people I knew from back home. When I saw you with those men at the ford I thought you'd gone to the Crossing for help to run us out and," she flushed, "I was getting set to shoot you out of the saddle, then you came close enough that I could see you were tied on the horse and beaten up. I watched the direction they took you and saw it wasn't toward the bowl and I got curious. I waited until you were all out of sight and followed the tracks. I came up behind that ridge in time to see them stopped here, cutting you loose, manhandling you like animals, so I hid there and waited until they left. I stayed there until I was sure they hadn't seen me, had pretended to ride out and meant to sneak back and catch me too. When I thought it was safe I came down."

Bentley made the effort to smile at her, as widely as his cracked mouth would let him stretch it. "I never met a guardian angel face to face before. I'm Cal Bentley. That's Dude Harris, my foreman and crew."

"I'm Sally Roebuck, we're from Tennessee, the whole wagon train, and the men plan to work on the dam when they start building."

"If they start . . . ever." Bentley's bitterness was sharp in his voice.

She rocked back on her heels, shocked. "If . . . what do you mean?"

"You're new here so you probably don't know about the fight. Boss Herbert, the man who had us brought here to die, is the only rancher in Snakeshead Valley and he wants to keep it that way."

"Yes, I've heard that, but if the court ruled his claim isn't legal and it's all government land how does he think he can hold it?"

"He thinks he's God. He can't keep the people at bay forever . . . Sooner or later there'll be enough federal men brought in to force Herbert out. But until they come there's no one in the country with power enough to do it."

"The law has power. What about the sheriff?"

"He quit."

"Won't they get another one?"

"They did last night. Me. That's why you saw me tied on a horse and ridden out here. Did you see anyone . . . anyone at all, try to stop it?"

Her puzzled eyes told him she did not understand and he explained, "The Crossing people are so cowed by Boss Herbert they'll walk around four blocks to keep from meeting him. As soon as he learned I had been appointed he came to town with part of his crew and gathered Dude and me in. With us gone there is no one to serve the formal court order, no one strong enough to push him out of that valley."

She was no less puzzled than before, watching his face closely. "You didn't think you could beat him alone, just the two of you?"

"No." His discouragement made the word sour in his mouth. "We can't. And I don't know where to get deputies in a hurry. I'd have to look for them in other counties and that would take too much time."

She surprised him by laughing. "I'll get them for you. How many do you want?"

He knew what she had in mind, her people, the farmers he had already discounted, and his mouth twisted. "You don't really believe the shack town men would go up against Boss Herbert, do you?"

"I do. For a very good reason. We all came out here early to work on the dam and when the irrigation district is established to take up land and build homes, make a living. If Herbert is permitted to get away with blocking the dam we'll all starve. There is no other work here, no useable land. There is no other choice."

His first strange reaction was an urge to laugh. There was nothing funny in the situation, but he was picturing Boss Herbert's face if he heard that Cal Bentley was not only alive but was coming with men at his back. He looked across at Dude Harris and saw the little rider's head swinging sideways like a metronome, saying as clearly as words that it was a vain, forlorn hope. He thought so himself and tried to get it across to this spunky, feisty girl.

46

"It would be rough, really hairy. Boss is fighting for his life and he's got a big crew. Fifteen to twenty and they are very rough characters. They'll fight. They love to fight, just for the fun of it. Farmers, storekeepers . . . they're not used to that."

She stood up, straightening, making herself as tall as possible, and looked down on him squarely. Her voice was sure and strong.

"They have fought. You can't know how well because you don't know mountain folk. Our crowd picked up and left because we were tired of a feud that kept us fighting for years, generations. We could have kept it up. We weren't beaten, we just decided we were tired of it and wanted a peaceful place to live." She raised her eyes to the western horizon, the sun nearly touching it. "First though I have to figure a way to get us back to the river with only one horse."

He admired the girl and her faith and in spite of his doubts he began to consider talking to her people, making what assessment he could of them, but as she said, he had to get to them before anything else. He said,

"Neither Dude nor I could walk far. I think we'd better wait here, if you'll go bring horses and help."

Her eyes narrowed and she tilted her head. "I will, but let's get you moved to another place in case that crowd comes back."

"They won't for awhile, they'll want to give us plenty of time to die."

"Maybe so, but that's careless thinking. I wouldn't want them to give you a nasty surprise. If you can get over to that trench I can let you down on my rope. There's probably an undercut at a bend, a washout you could stay in out of sight. I'll go see."

She walked toward the rim, a little kid, he thought, hardly bigger than a minute, the evening wind blowing the yellow hair around her head in a cloud that caught the last rays of the sun. She came back nodding in satisfaction.

"Right over there, only maybe three hundred feet. Can you get Dude up while I bring the horse?"

Harris gave her a laugh contemptuous of himself. "Missy, I'd never get in a saddle tonight."

"If you can stand, if you can move your legs, you can hang onto a stirrup and let the horse drag you, can't you?"

They worked it that way, Dude wrapping one arm through the stirrup and clamping his hands around his wrists, taking steps that bore no weight. Cal Bentley walked at his side but his legs were giving out, his knees shaking by the time they reached the rim. He and Dude sat down there while Bentley tied the girl's rope under the rider's armpits and she snugged the other end around the horn. Cal eased Dude over the edge and the girl brought the horse forward until Dude hollered up from twenty feet below that he was down.

Harris got out of the rope, threw it free and Bentley drew it up to bind around himself. Another call came up from Harris.

"Yippee . . . we got a nice cave under here, snug as you please." The words ended weakly, as if Harris had defiantly used the last of his strength in the effort.

"Sally," Bentley said, "you'll do to take along. I don't know another way to say thank you."

She shrugged. "Who do you think I'm helping? You or us? Get along down and I'll be back first thing in the morning."

Bentley went over the edge, swinging, holding himself off from the wall, smiling to himself. She had a chip on her shoulder, but it had not been her people she intended to help when she gave water to a man who had tried to rim her off his place.

At the bottom he shook the rope free and in the shadowy light down there saw her reel it in. Dude was already inside the shallow undercut, lying on his face, unmoving. Bentley went to his knees and began to crawl toward him, then he heard metal scraping against the wall and looked up. Sally Roebuck was sending down her rifle and the canteen.

If, in the darkness that would have fallen before she could get out of the lava, her horse went lame, put a hoof in a hole and wrenched a leg, she would be in deep trouble herself.

Bentley called to her to keep the water and gun. She did not answer, only threw her end of the rope over the rim, then he heard the horse moving away, the iron shoes clinking, the sound dying.

He retrieved the gifts and crawled in to Dude, rolling him on his back.

"You feeling worse for the hike?"

Dude Harris lay with his eyes closed and said without opening them, "I'm all right."

He was not all right. The quaver of weakness was in his tone and he was holding himself stiffly as if afraid to let go.

"Want some water?"

"Yeah."

Bentley lifted Dude's head and held the canteen to his lips. Some of the water ran into his mouth, most of it spilled down his chin and chest.

They slept then. Bentley dreamed in agony that he was trying to escape Boss Herbert's crew, racing up a canyon that quit suddenly in a high, solid stone face impossible to climb. He heard their horses closing in and turned, his back to the wall, his holster empty.

The horse sounds came closer and crowded through his nightmare, into his consciousness. They were real sounds. He waked, the dream terror clinging to him, and grabbed for the rifle at his side even before he opened his eyes.

The sky was light, bringing day down into the cut though it was still dim in the undercut. He lay quiet, holding his breath. Then the girl called. He relaxed, just discovering how tense he had been. He glanced at Dude Harris, still asleep, grey faced but breathing, then Cal crawled out of the shelter and stood up. He was stiff in his joints and he ached, but he felt much better, almost whole. He stepped out from the wall and raised his head to see the rim.

Sally Roebuck's blond head showed there, and men lined along the edge on either side of her. Once she had seen him she stepped back out of sight and a little later the rope snaked out and dropped near his feet. Before he touched it he called.

"I'll have to have help with Dude, he's not good."

A man's voice answered. "Fetch yourself up, then we'll git him."

He tied the rope under his arms and when it drew taut put his feet against the wall, leaned back and walked up as the horse pulled him higher. At the top hands reached for him, caught the hands he held up and hoisted him to the ground. The man on his right was the tall, dour one he had told to get out of the bowl. Others took the rope off him and two went down with a blanket. Cal kept hold of the tall man's hand, squeezing it.

"Mister, I am glad to see you. Oh, am I glad to see you."

He turned his foot on a stone and stumbled and Sally caught his arm, both she and the man steadying him, the girl saying quickly,

"Here, sit down on this rock. You're still weak." When he was seated she indicated the man. "This is my paw, Josh Roebuck, and that's my uncle Seth. The rest here are friends and relatives. They want to help."

Cal Bentley felt a hot flush of embarrassment and Josh Roebuck saw it, shook Bentley's hand once and let it drop. He kicked at the ground with a boot toe and spoke in a rueful tone.

"It's all right, Mister . . . you was in your rights . . . we was told wrong. My Sal says you're looking for some deputies."

Before Bentley could answer Seth said from Sally's side, "What's this sheriffing job pay in these parts?"

The county commissioners had paid. Brandy Ives fifty dollars a month and his deputies thirty each, but in view of what lay ahead for these men should they take on the fight, Bentley believed the risks they would take were worth more, a lot more. He said without hesitation,

"A hundred a month a man. You furnish your own guns and horses." If the men who held the county purse strings balked Cal would make up the difference himself.

"A hundred . . ." Seth Roebuck shouted it incredulously, as if he did not believe there was that much money in the world. "Son, you just hired yourself a hand. You just hired fifteen hands . . . How about it boys?"

The mountain men had gathered around to listen, dour faced, work-worn people in patched pants and shirts and cracking leather boots and their mouths dropped open as if on command. Then suddenly they were waving their hats in the air and cackling, dancing clumsily, pounding each other on the shoulders. Behind them Bentley saw the man at the rim with the horse used to lift the rope lead it off and heard him call for help in raising Dude Harris. Everyone ran to lend a hand and as Dude's limp form came up, the rope under his arms and the arms tied against his sides to hold it there, the mountain men caught him and hoisted him onto the lava cap, laying him down with unexpected gentleness. Harris groaned in weak relief.

Josh Roebuck turned his attention back to Bentley, patting his rifle. "Now, Sheriff, what's the orders?"

Cal Bentley's eyes stayed on Dude Harris and worry for the rider was his first concern.

"We have to get him to the ranch where One Lung can take care of him."

"Who?"

"My Chinese cook. The name's a joke. I never heard his real one."

The girl laughed but the men looked at him unblinking, showing no humor. Sally sobered and said,

"I think Dude needs a doctor. Wouldn't it be wiser to take him to town?"

Bentley raised his head to look at her. "Boss Herbert and his crew could be there . . ."

"So," said Josh Roebuck, "will we. We'll look after it."

"Let's go then," Bentley told him, "lift him up in the saddle with me."

Josh Roebuck raised a farmer's look at the sky where the sun was already beginning to make itself felt, then spat at the ground.

"Gonna be a warm ride and you don't look to me awful mighty yourself. Best let Seth take him up. His horse is bigger."

Bentley smiled and let the man see it. The mention of the bigger horse was a nice piece of diplomacy to take the sting out of the fact that Cal Bentley was in no condition to support Dude Harris through the long ride. "Appreciate that," he said and turned toward one of the extra animals the men had brought along.

53

The girl rode at Bentley's side, ostensibly to pass him bread and meat to gnaw on, water to drink, the first food he had had since the morning before, but he suspected that her main purpose was to watch that the increasing heat did not weaken him further, make him dizzy enough to fall out of the saddle. He decided that he had drastically underestimated all these people.

Doc Morey, ever since Cal could remember, had been threatening to leave the Crossing, but he was still there, a thin, cranky man with a high bridged nose pinched between the clips of his half-moon spectacles. He examined Dude, making an angry whinny every time he found another abrasion or broken bone. When he finished he straightened, took off the glasses and rubbed the red spots they left on his nose.

"If a man did this to me I'd kill him."

"I am going to," Dude said. He had had three stiff drinks from the Doc's medicinal bottle of whiskey and was looking and acting better, deliberately cocky.

"First we set the arm," Morey told Harris. "Then we take a few tucks in that skull, then we put you to bed."

Dude snorted. "Doc, you know I'm not about to stay in bed in the daytime . . . I . . ."

"You are. If I have to tie you down or chloroform you."

Cal Bentley had been watching the street through the dirty window. Doc Morey lived alone and the three second floor rooms that he used as office, kitchen and sleeping quarters were never cleaned except when a group of townswomen grew sufficiently incensed to make a mass invasion, override his indignation and take the place apart. Bentley turned to the table where Harris was just sitting up.

"All right if I take him to the ranch?"

"It is not all right." Morey sounded huffy. "He's still in shock. Take him to the hotel."

"Where Herbert's crowd can work him over again?"

"Give him a gun. I'd judge Dude can shoot better lying down than Boss Herbert can standing up."

"You're damn right I can." Dude worked the fingers of his unbroken left hand. "Let me get that critter lined up in my sights and I'll shoot him to pieces. First his fingers, one at a time, then his toes, then . . ."

Cal Bentley said sharply, "Lady present."

Sally Roebuck had just opened the door and stepped in. Harris discovered her and flushed a dark crimson and Doc Morey snapped at her.

"You get out of here, girl. I'm working on him. Send some muscle up here in a half hour to cart him out."

Josh and Seth Roebuck reported when Dude's head was stitched and his right arm set, his cuts and scratches patched. They made a chair of their arms and Dude sat on them, his good arm around Seth's neck while they carried him down the outside stairs and along the street to the hotel.

Billy Boils, the clerk, was not happy to see them come in. He skittered around to Bentley, behind them, and said in a swift undertone,

"Get him out of here. Get him out of town. Boss and his boys rode in awhile ago. In the saloon now. If they find Dude . . ."

Bentley brushed past him, went to the key rack, took the key to room number ten and nodded to the Roebucks to carry Harris up to the second floor. Sally had followed them into the lobby and told Bentley,

"I'll go up and sit with him and make him behave."

Cal nodded, saying nothing, his mouth set in a tight line. He watched the little troupe until they were out of sight in the upper hall, then he turned on his heel, crossed to the connecting door and walked into the saloon.

CHAPTER
SIX

Cal Bentley stood in the doorway relaxing his muscles, having his look around the room filled with townsmen and ranchers, marking their disposal. The long ride back to town and the time it had taken Doc Morey to do all that was needed for Dude Harris had eaten the day. The lingering twilight was fading outside and in the saloon the lamps were burning above the gaming tables and the bar.

Boss Herbert sat at a rear poker game, his back to the corner where he could observe all that went on. He glanced up as movement at the lobby door caught his attention and saw Cal Bentley standing there quietly. As if a heavy blow had driven into his chest he slammed back against his chair, then sat frozen. Under the yellow light that fell on him his deep tan looked sallow. He opened and closed his mouth again and again like a gasping fish, then with slow deliberation he stood up.

The players facing Herbert could not see Bentley, did not know what Herbert's action meant but they recognized danger and dived out of the line of possible fire. Bentley's hard eyes had already found the foreman Joe Garvey and one other Box H rider at the bar, leaning on it, their shoulders hunched over it supporting their weight on their arms. Neither noticed Herbert's move nor knew Bentley was there until Herbert's strangled voice cut at them.

"Joe . . . Rowley . . ."

Turning their heads to see what he wanted they read the shock on his face, saw the direction he was looking and spun on around. Both men swore and crouched, more as if their legs were collapsing than if they intended it. Then Garvey's hand started a slap toward his gun that stopped when he saw the weapons already in Bentley's hands, one trained on Boss Herbert, the other on the riders. Bentley's cold voice sliced across at them.

"Don't touch it, Joe. I don't want to have to kill you for resisting arrest."

Joe Garvey stared, then straightened and started a laugh. "Arrest . . . ? For what?"

"Kidnapping and attempted murder."

The foreman was recovering, his thin lips pulling back against his teeth in a wicked grin.

"Now who's going to back you up? You fool enough to think you can march in here all alone and pull me out?"

"I'm doing it. Turn around."

"Hell with you."

Cal Bentley's gun exploded. The bullet sped between Garvey's legs, rang against the brass rail and ricocheted. A card player across the room yelped, hit in the leg by the spent lead.

"Turn." Bentley was savage. "Next shot will be two feet higher."

Garvey turned.

"You," Bentley told the other Box H man, "lift your gun with one finger and drop it, then do the same with Garvey's."

The man was slow, debating the risk of trying and Bentley's muzzle moved the fraction to train on him. The rider used a crooked forefinger to edge his gun butt high enough to spill the gun to the floor, then walked around Garvey to take his and drop it.

"Keep going," Bentley said, "over by Herbert." And when the rider stopped beside the rear table he told Garvey, "Come over here, backward."

Boss Herbert still stood rigidly in front of his chair, his teeth clenched tight and his jaw muscles bulging. He said through his teeth.

"You will never get out of town alive."

"Why," said Cal Bentley, "if it seems so I'll at least take a lot of company with me. Keep coming, Joe."

The foreman turned his glance toward the rancher for instruction. Boss Herbert told him,

"Go along, Joe. We won't leave you in that jailhouse for long."

Bentley could see the side of Garvey's face as he grinned, then the man was close and Cal took two backward steps into the lobby and as Garvey came through the doorway holstered one gun, raised the other and cracked it hard behind the foreman's ear.

Garvey began to crumple. Bentley caught him, bent and slung him over his shoulder and ran. He made the short detour to slam open the front door of the hotel, seeing the clerk duck down behind his high desk, seeing the Roebuck brothers coming down, near the bottom of the stairs and waving them along with him. Then he was across the lobby and through the door to the dining room.

It was too early for the supper hour and there was no one at the tables there, no lamps yet lighted. He raced for the kitchen door, hearing behind him the yells and noise of Boss Herbert and his riders charging across the saloon, men pouring out of its front entrance to waylay him on the street. His decoy slamming of the hotel door had worked for the moment but there was no time to spare.

With the Roebucks behind him he ran through the lighted kitchen where the cook and two waitresses were busy at the stove and work tables, dodged around the women and flung out to the dim alley. There the tall, long legged Josh Roebuck caught up with him.

"The livery . . . The boys are there."

Keeping a tight hold on the unconscious Garvey, Bentley sprinted along the rutted dust to the side street and turned into that, following the poles of the livery corral. In the barn runway his new deputies were gathered, out of the light of the single lamp in the bracket beside the office. Bentley dumped the foreman on the thin hay in the nearest box stall and straightened, breathless.

Filling his lungs, talking as he exhaled, he said, "Send somebody . . . guard . . . Harris . . . Don't let

... anybody in ... that room. Number ten ... upstairs."

Josh Roebuck beckoned to a lanky redhead in his early twenties. "Scott South, Sheriff ... Scott, you heard him, take your Greening and blow the head off anybody that tries."

The redhead grinned and shook the long gun in front of himself. "Be a pleasure, Sheriff." He rolled away with a swift, gimpy, angling gait, one leg somewhat shorter than the other. There seemed to Bentley a frailty about the boy, and after his riding out to the Burning Land in the early morning, the hot ride back, he wondered about Scott South's stamina and asked Josh Roebuck,

"He won't fall asleep on the job?"

Roebuck grunted. "Scott would stay awake a week for the chance he might get to shoot that iron of his."

"I just pray he doesn't have to. Now pick a couple of men to hog tie and gag Garvey and haul him up in the hay mow out of sight. Tell them to tie him to a post so he can't roll to the edge, and then join us. The rest of us will go see Boss Herbert."

Huey Ellis, the night stable man, had not put his head out of his office door. He was an old timer at the Crossing and did not like the new people ... squatters, he called them, and if they wanted something of him they would have to come to him and ask. He paid no attention to the action in the runway and so did not see Joe Garvey trussed and carried up the ladder, did not see Bentley lead the dozen farmers out to the street.

At Bentley's direction the bulk of them crossed on over to the opposite sidewalk while he, flanked by Josh Roebuck and another man turned back toward the hotel. It was dark now and he made out a darker block of men still clustered around the hotel door with the burly figure of Boss Herbert in the middle, lighted by the yellow rectangle that shone out. Herbert was shouting mad, drumming up a mob to storm the jail, and support was growing, the riders and town people not daring to defy the rancher.

Herbert discovered Cal Bentley and stopped his harangue short and the group around him swung about, saw the trio coming and spread in a semi-circle leaving Herbert at the center. Bentley walked steadily, quickly toward them. They stood off balance. Here was something they did not understand. They had expected him to try to reach the jail and barricade himself with his prisoner inside.

Bentley stopped twenty feet away, his guns holstered and making no move to draw them. Instead he called,

"Before you start something, Boss, something you can't finish, take a look across the street."

All attention had been on Bentley's advance. No one had noticed the small crowd led by Seth Roebuck that had moved parallel to Bentley through the shadows of the opposite buildings. If anyone had been aware of them they had assumed they were coming in to listen to Boss Herbert. Now everyone turned their way and looked into a line of shotguns and rifles as Seth's men stepped into the lighter area at the edge of the side-walk. Boss Herbert's voice, heavy with arrogance, carried across the dusty street.

"Who the hell are you? Sing out. Move on, this is not your business."

"It is their business," Bentley called. "They are my sworn deputies. Box H, throw down your guns and the rest of you clear out. Herbert, you are under arrest and will be held for trial."

There was a stunned silence around the rancher, then the crowd began melting away, people who had little taste for being in the middle of the gunplay they expected to erupt. Within one minute the street in front of the hotel was empty except for Herbert and his riders. Herbert was shouting curses across the way.

"You damn ground grubbers are crazy. I'm going to make this country so hot for you you'll scorch your pants seats getting out of it. All right, Box H, let the guns go for now."

Boss Herbert had only four riders with him and they did not like the odds. They threw their guns away and raised their hands shoulder high as the two parties of deputies converged around them. Cal Bentley went to meet Seth Roebuck in the middle of the street, saying.

"Nice and clean, Seth. We'll walk them down to the jail now."

Boss Herbert was the last to move. He stood sneering, swaggering, bawling at the top of his voice.

"Lawyer feller, what do you think you're pulling with this grandstand play?"

Bentley said in a flat, cold tone, "Walk, Boss, and I'll tell you on the way," and when Herbert started along the sidewalk Cal added, "first I am going to serve you with the court order to vacate Snakeshead Valley. Then I am going out and burn your buildings, tear out your fences and throw your cattle up in the high hills. If you can identify them when you come out of prison you're welcome to take them anyplace you want . . . except the valley."

Herbert gave him a growling laugh. "Just what makes you think you can put me in prison?"

"You put yourself there, Boss, when you left Dude and me in the Burning Land without water or horses and beat up to boot."

The big man cursed steadily all the way to the jail behind the courthouse. At the cell Seth Roebuck put his shotgun barrel in the rancher's back and prodded him through the grille, locked it after him with a key on the ring Bentley handed him. They locked the riders in the only other cell, then Bentley stayed to watch over them while part of his group went to the livery for Joe Garvey. He was brought in conscious, balky, and thunderstruck when he saw Boss Herbert through the bars, a rigid figure sitting on one bunk with his back turned toward the hall. Garvey was put in the second cell with the riders. Bentley stood outside Herbert's cell and read the court order to vacate Snakeshead Valley, with plenty of witnesses. Then, except for Garvey, the Box H riders were brought out, sullen and glowering.

Cal Bentley told them, "Take your horses and get out of here. If I see one of you in the Valley or the Crossing again I'll haul you up on the same charges Herbert is going to face. Believe it."

64

They stalked out, their haste making it evident that they did not trust this bit of luck and wanted to be away before this man who was not afraid of Boss might change his mind. Josh watched after them, uneasy.

"Letting them go . . . They'll head for the ranch and tip our hand. I don't mind a fight but I'd like to make it a surprise."

Bentley shrugged. "I don't think they will. They had a scare tonight and they're just riders. Without Herbert or Garvey they probably haven't got much stomach for a war."

Bentley and Josh followed them to the street and watched as they hurried to their horses, hitched back at the saloon rail, saw them mount and ride off fast, heading south, away from Snakeshead Valley. Josh nodded doubtfully and Bentley grinned at him.

"So far it's beautiful. Next move is to the ranch. You and Seth stand guard here, spell each other, get what sleep you can. I'm going to check on Dude, then I'll take your people with me . . . be back in the morning."

Josh toed the ground and spat, disappointed. "Couldn't a couple of the boys stay? They'll all do what you say but I sort of hate to get left out."

Bentley gave him a grave look. "It's very important here. There's the banker, Allen, in town and he sides with Herbert. It might be he'd try to break him out with a mob, but you two could hold this office. There are only the one door and window. I'd feel better with you and Seth on deck."

"Oh. That case it's different. You go on and I'll have the boys get your horse with theirs and pick you up at the saloon."

Through his single-minded purpose an inspiration flashed on Bentley and he dug in his pocket for money, held it out to Roebuck.

"Here, let them get a round of drinks to ride on. They're having a long day."

He turned away quickly from the proud mountain man's embarrassment and went to the hotel by the rear door and up the rear stairs. The saloon would be full of men, loud with gossip about the arrest and if Able Allen were there Bentley did not want him connecting Dude with the hotel.

The successes of the day had wiped away his tiredness, given him a second wind and an eagerness to reach Herbert's ranch. He took the stairs two at a time but stopped abruptly as his head came above the upper floor level. He was looking up the long muzzle of Scott South's beloved Greening. There was a tight pleasure on the thin face that faded in a comic wipe when he recognized the lawyer and there was a small boy's disgust in his tone.

"Aw, shucks . . ."

Bentley could not help laughing as he went on up, then he held out a bone. "Sorry, Scott, but that was a good job, and you may still get a crack at somebody tonight."

He went on by to the door of number ten, rapped lightly and opened it. The lamp inside was turned low, Sally Roebuck sitting quietly in a straight backed chair beside the bed. The Dude was asleep, his deeply tanned, lined face showing gaunt after the ordeal. The girl stood up and came to the door to answer the question in Bentley's raised eyebrows, whispering.

"Doc says what he needs most is sleep. He gave him some laudanum."

"No use your sitting up then. Go on next door and rest. I'll fix it with the desk tomorrow."

She did not argue, went back for the lamp and carried it to number nine, waiting there while Bentley closed Dude's door and joined her. With Scott South an interested audience on his chair against the wall she asked,

"Are you going to sleep here too?"

"No, we're riding to the Box H to burn it and rip out the fences, scatter the cattle."

"Tonight? When you're so worn out? I don't think that's a smart way to start a war."

He smiled at her and winked over at Scott South. "General, my strategy is to avoid war. Boss Herbert and Joe Garvey are in jail and there's no one to lead their crew. When they see the strength we have I figure they'll pull out without trouble. Why should they fight for a ranch that's closed down?"

She nodded slowly, looking back through her memories, sounding uncertain. "Yes . . . I've seen that happen in the feuds. One side would pull back. But then they always regrouped and started in again . . . Are Paw and Uncle Seth going with you?"

"They're staying to guard the jail in case somebody tries to break my prisoners out. If you need anything you can find them there. Good night . . . and many thanks for all your help. None of this would have been possible without you, Sally."

She stayed in the hall until he was out of sight down the back stairs, his running steps surprisingly light. She thought that she had never known anyone like Cal Bentley. Unlike the young mountain men she knew, he was educated, which her people had always distrusted. Too much book learning, they believed, softened and weakened a man's natural abilities, but there was neither softness nor weakness about this lawyer. He had taken on the biggest ranch she had ever heard of single-handed, even before she had brought him the men to back him up. She smiled secretly, feeling a strange glow at his last words to her.

It was a long hour's ride to the Box H and Cal Bentley used the time to get acquainted, learn the men's names, and to go over his plan with his unlikely deputies. He did not expect anyone at the ranch to be up by the time they got there, and when they turned into the mile-long lane he was reassured to see no lights in any of the buildings.

As they rode under the wide timber arch, the symbolic gate, he slowed his men to a walk to lessen the chance of alerting any light sleeper in the bunkhouse that so many were coming. Some noise could be put down to the homecoming of Herbert and the few with him. He did not know how many he would find, but he wanted to take control without bloodletting if possible.

In the ranch yard Bentley dismounted his people and left one man with the horses and made a last review of the tactics.

"That's the bunkhouse, over beyond the cookshack. Everyone on the ranch should be in there. Surround the building, at least one man on every window and the rest at the door. Jed, you and Lem come with me. We'll go inside. If we're all very quiet we may be lucky enough to get a lamp lighted before they wake up."

The group split, half easing around the building one way, the rest the other until they met at the rear. When they had had time to get in place Bentley eased the door open, testing for creaking hinges, but it moved silently and he stepped through, his footfalls soft as he moved to one side to let the others follow. In the heavy dark the only sound was the irregular breathing of the Box H crew.

He struck a match on his thumbnail, spotted a lamp in a wall bracket close beside him, lifted the smoked chimney and lit the wick, replacing the chimney. Someone in the bunks stirred and growled.

"Christ, Garvey, can't you find your way without that light?"

Bentley growled back a wordless sound, raised his gun and put a bullet through the low roof. Men rolled up, rolled out to their feet, eyes filled with sleep and minds dulled and stood bewildered, stunned, gaping at him. He leveled the gun down and from the corner of his eye saw Jed and Lem swing their rifles to cover the room.

"Stand quiet." Bentley's voice was a whip crack. "Look at the windows."

They continued blinking at him, then slowly the heads turned. Through every window, open to the summer night, rifle barrels were thrust, held steady by men whose faces were half hidden behind the sights, barely revealed by the light that filtered outside.

"I wouldn't advise any wild ideas about being heroes. Lem, Jed, go around and collect their arms."

One of the men, in red underwear like the rest, swore at him. "Boss will skin you alive, shyster."

"Boss and Joe both are in jail. Stay still and you won't be hurt." His cold voice hung in the air while the two boys gathered guns, belts, holsters from the pegs on the bunk posts and piled them against the blank rear wall, and when they came back beside Bentley he said in the same hard tone, "Now get dressed to ride."

The one who had spoken before snarled, "What the hell do you think you're doing?"

"Getting rid of the ranch. You have ten minutes to dress, pick up your gear and clear out of here. If you are found in the territory tomorrow you will be shot."

It was the same kind of threat Boss Herbert had often used and they had enforced, running people off property they had an equal right to use, and because of that they believed Bentley. They scrambled for their clothes, muttering but hurrying none the less.

CHAPTER
SEVEN

In the darkness the mountain men marched the Box H crew to the corral and held them under the long guns while they saddled and rode out, then sped them on their way with shots over their heads. The riders stayed not on the order of their going, went galloping out of the yard. Cal Bentley thought he need not worry that they might turn back.

Under his direction the new deputies spread coal oil through the headquarters building, the bunkhouse, barns and sheds and set the fires. In a very little time the ranch was blazing, bright flames licking up the sun-dried wood, lighting the yard with an angry red glow that picked out running figures and cast grotesque shadows dancing after them.

The lawyer watched the inferno and sighed deeply. Here was the end of the Box H, the culmination of the long fight he and Colonel Ruggles had waged for the irrigation district.

In the morning they would pull out the fences and haze the cattle into the side canyons, but for the rest of this night they would roll in the blankets salvaged from the bunkhouse for a rest they all had earned.

Bentley chose a grassy knoll out of reach of the searing heat and had just stretched out. The house roof fell in with a crashing roar, throwing a fountain of sparks and new flame high in a final display. Then as the noise subsided the sound of a running horse drummed over it. Bentley rolled up to look down the lane and call a warning to the men. He could not believe a Box H rider was driving back at such a hellbent pace, but who else might it be.

Out of the blackness beyond the reach of firelight a horse came rushing. Bentley leveled his rifle on it, then lowered it and ran to meet it. Sally Roebuck veered toward him and pulled the lathered animal to a dancing stop and threw herself out of the saddle at his side.

His first fear was that someone had gotten to Dude Harris, but there was too much desperation in the face that reflected the red flames. He waited while she gasped for breath to speak, while the men ran in around her, then heard her cry.

"My father . . . my uncle . . . Paw's dead and Uncle Seth nearly is."

"Sally . . . How?" Bentley caught her shoulders, holding her up as she swayed.

She spoke with deliberate control, fighting a hysteria that crowded close to the surface. "You hadn't been gone an hour when I heard an explosion. A big one. I was afraid it would start a fire, and got dressed to go find out. It was the jail office. Somebody blew it up . . ."

Her voice broke and she could not go on, then, forcing herself, she said, "People were running to the courthouse. I asked a man who was already there what had happened and he told me dynamite must have been thrown in the window. It went off under my father's chair. It blew him to pieces and hurt Uncle Seth badly."

Cal Bentley swore steadily under his breath. The settler Lem swore aloud.

"Who was it, Sally? Does anybody know?"

She nodded, choking, then went on in a rush. "Uncle Seth saw him at the window before he threw a package. He described him to Doctor Morey. The doctor said it sounded like Able Allen. After the explosion the man charged into the office, took the keys and let Boss Herbert and his foreman out of the cells and they all ran out before anyone came."

Fear for Harris rushed back and Bentley said sharply, "Is the South boy still watching Dude?"

"Yes, and the doctor had Uncle Seth carried to the hotel and put in the next room. Morey promised to stay with them until you can get to town."

Bentley raised his voice for the men with the order to mount up, to ride for the Crossing. The fences, the cattle would have to wait. With Boss Herbert and Joe Garvey loose there was too much danger that they might find Dude. He ran for his horse while Lem helped the girl back to her saddle and led them at a steady run toward the town.

Bentley did not remember the ride. His mind was too full of the new problems. He had been confident that with the Box H leader behind bars the fight against Herbert was won. Now with the rancher and his foreman outside it would start all over. He hoped the crew they had run off had ridden far enough that Herbert could not find them, but in the same instant knew the hope was vain. More likely they had only ridden off the ranch and camped. They would have no reason to hurry once they were out of Bentley's sight. Herbert would probably make contact with them by morning. He might have already found them. Bentley slowed, letting the crew come up and warning them that it was possible they would ride into a fight at the Crossing.

They went in cautiously but when they splashed across the ford there was no sign of Box H men. The main street was still full of people, the bars crowded, everyone speculating on what Boss Herbert would do next, and people on the sidewalks turned to follow Cal Bentley's watchful parade.

They rode first to Able Allen's house, found it dark and empty looking, but Bentley wanted to make sure. He sent his men to cover the sides and rear, then kicked the front door in. There was no one there and Allen's guns were gone. Outside, the horses the banker kept in his corral were also gone, indicating that Allen had ridden out with Boss Herbert and Joe Garvey.

Bentley swung back into his saddle and led the mountain men to the hotel. They dismounted again there, the men pushing into the saloon, and Bentley and the girl went on up the stairs. Scott South greeted them with his Greening leveled, disappointed again that this was not his chance to avenge the violence against his leaders.

74

They went first to the room where Seth Roebuck lay in a stupor and Doc Morey sat in a chair propped back against the wall with a shotgun across his knees. Bentley called before he opened the door and the doctor, knowing who was there, did not move from his position. The girl went at once to the bed, saying,

"Is he going to be all right, Doctor?"

Morey's voice was astringent. "He's got a slight concussion from being blown across the room against the wall. He ought to be fine in three or four days if he rests."

"And Dude?" Bentley asked.

"Tough old rooster. Another man would have gone out but he'll manage it unless something else happens to him."

"I mean to see that nothing does. I'm putting two men at the bottom of the stairs and add another up here. In case Boss Herbert tries to get at him again."

The doctor squinted at him. "You get some rest yourself, boy. You look like a mild case of death warmed over. Take a couple of slugs of whiskey, drink them fast so you knock yourself out. You too, missy, you can't do anybody any good if you wear yourself clear down."

"Later," Bentley told him. "First I have to find out if anyone knows where Herbert and Garvey and Allen went, then I have to talk to the county commissioners. Are you staying here?"

Morey straightened the chair and got to his feet. "I've got more people than these two to look after and I've learned the sense to sleep when I need it. I see you're going to give me an argument about somebody being with your uncle, girl, so get a blanket from another room and curl up on the floor. I swear I'm going to move out of this loco place and go where people use their heads for something besides butting against stone walls. Good night."

Morey stomped out and when Sally had brought bedding Bentley went down to the lobby. The mountain men had had their drink and were clustered at the bottom of the stairs waiting for orders. Bentley detailed three to keep watch, sent the others to the livery to bed down in the hay and chose four to relieve the guard when they had had three hours sleep. As they were leaving Moses Foster and Morton Thompson crowded past them coming in from the street, hurrying.

Thompson spotted Bentley and planted himself in front of the lawyer, panting. "See you, Cal?"

"I was on my way to hunt you up. Does anybody know where Herbert went?"

"How the hell would we?" Foster was belligerent. "You sure raised hell as sheriff . . . All you managed was to get the jail wrecked."

Anger rose to gorge Bentley. Neither of these commissioners cared that Josh Roebuck had been killed, that Seth was badly hurt or that Dude Harris was fighting for his life. To them the mountain men were foreigners, ignorant riff-raff come here to work on a dam neither of them wanted and to take up land Boss Herbert claimed. His outrage made his tone icy.

"I am not finished quite yet. I am going to put out a warrant for Able Allen for that explosion, charging him with murder."

76

Foster sneered. "What do you think Herbert and the Box H will be doing while you're chasing Allen?"

"If they know what's good for them they'll keep running. I have twenty men aching for a crack at those killers."

"That trash? They won't stand up for one minute when Box H comes at them . . . Another thing . . . who do you expect to pay these hillbillies?"

"The county."

Thompson shook a finger in Bentley's face. "Not while I am a commissioner, not for one single second. Far as I'm concerned they can hitch their wagons and haul out of here. The sooner the better. And you, Bentley, I'd just as soon you turned in that star. Now."

Cal Bentley pulled himself up, his face hard, his smile hard. "Not until I have cleared this up. Take me to court or do anything you damn please, but as sheriff of this county the only man who can remove me is the governor, and he is not going to pull your chestnuts out of the fire. Morton, you're just afraid of Boss Herbert."

"If you had half the sense God gave a goose you would be too . . . you'd be clearing out of this country fast as a horse can carry you."

"I never learned how to run."

"The time's coming when you'll wish you had."

Bentley fought to keep his patience, saying evenly, "You two are betting on the wrong side. Boss Herbert is licked. He can't fight the federal government and if he tries there'll be so many federal marshals here they'll block the street. Keep that in mind, and now leave me alone."

They sputtered for a moment longer, then marched out of the lobby in a huff. Bentley watched them go, breathing deeply, trying to cool himself, and when he had his anger in hand he crossed to the bar.

At the long counter he signaled for a bottle, noting that all conversation had stopped when he came in. He looked at the mirror, seeing that men on both sides of him watched him from the corners of their eyes. He turned slowly until he faced half of the room.

"Anyone got anything to say?"

He knew he was in an ugly mood and did not care. If someone wanted a fight at the moment he would be more than willing to oblige. But only silence answered him. He threw down the two quick drinks Morey had prescribed, spun a half-dollar on the bar and went out the front door to the street, heading for the livery and a stall near his deputies.

It was after three, would be light in an hour, but while the crowd had thinned there were still many more people on the sidewalks than was usual this late. The lantern was burning in the barn office, the door to the runway open and Huey Ellis sat at his old roll-top desk staring at nothing. He heard Cal, looked to see who was there, and hailed him with an urgent wave. As Cal stepped inside Huey said emphatically,

"I thought you was never going to show up. Come over here . . . Shut the door."

Bentley closed it and went to the desk in the corner of the littered room. Ellis tugged him down and spoke in a low voice close to his ear.

78

"I guess maybe I'm the only one in town with any idea where they went."

Tired as he was, feeling the two drinks and still fuming over Foster and Thompson, Bentley said, "Where who went?"

The barn man's voice was disgusted. "Who would I be meaning on this night? Who is anybody in town talking about? Boss Herbert. Joe Garvey. Able Allen. That's who."

Cal scrubbed at his temples with the heels of his hands. "I'm sorry, Huey, my mind's not too clear just now. Where did they head for?"

"Malcolm's Ferry."

"You sure?"

"I heard them, didn't I? Tell you how it was. When that blast at the courthouse let go I ran up there like everybody else. When we figured out what had happened I got to thinking. They'd need horses. One of them hillbillies you got working for you brought Herbert's and Garvey's animals here when you put them in jail and Boss don't like to ride anything but that big grey of his.

"I didn't say a word to nobody, there wasn't a man in this yellow town would raise a finger to stop them. I just moseyed on back here . . . Oh, I didn't come by the street, didn't want them to see me. I think too much of my neck. I stayed close in the shadows, come the back way. Time I got here they was already in the corral saddling up and talking. They talked low but I got good ears. Herbert was thanking Allen, then he said you'd probably run off his crew and burned his place . . . called you some real fancy names.

"Allen asked where he was going and Boss said to the Ferry, that the crew had probably gone that way and maybe he could catch them. He's aiming to hang and scalp everybody who had a hand in wrecking the ranch."

"All right, Huey. Thanks." Bentley was too tired to sound eager at the news.

The barn man was disappointed. "You ain't going to do nothing about it either?"

"I am going to do a good deal about it, but first I need sleep. Wake me at five. Rout out my men and herd them up to the hotel for breakfast, and for Pete sake don't tell anyone where we're going." Bentley dug a dollar out of his pocket and put it in Huey's calloused hand.

"I never even talked to you." Huey shook his head vigorously. "I never even thought about talking, believe me."

80

CHAPTER
EIGHT

In the pale early light they took the road southward toward Malcolm's Ferry, eighteen grim-faced men with Cal Bentley at their head. More than half of them were related to the Roebucks and the rest had followed Josh with deep respect. Cal could almost feel the bitter hatred that drove them now.

They were out to revenge their leaders and Bentley found himself feeling sorry for Herbert's crew. He had no sympathy for Herbert himself or Joe Garvey or Able Allen. The banker was a murderer as surely as if he had fired a gun at the Roebuck men. Joe Garvey was a professional gun who had hired out to one rancher after another before he landed with Box H, and Herbert had proved he would stop at nothing to get whatever he wanted. The crew was tough, some of them were outlaws, but they were still only riders, not makers of decisions.

It was a good twenty miles to the Ferry by the road that followed the curves of the river, a serpentine path between the two chains of hills that flanked the valley on either side. It was little used. They rode alert, watching the slopes and turns as they approached them, mindful that Herbert might have found his crew and set an ambush, but they saw no one in the whole empty stretch between the two communities.

It was nearing noon when they walked their horses over the last rise and looked down on the straggle of buildings that was Malcolm's Ferry. Bentley would have chosen surprise but the road dropped into a narrows of the canyon and ran against the brink of the river, so close that the water boiling over its rock bed splashed across the dirt track, putting them in plain sight of the town on the opposite bank.

It was a sorry town, its single street crowded against the far side of the river and sun warped, unpainted buildings in a row facing the road. The ferry raft was poled back and forth along a rope stretched to keep the water, thirty feet wide and fast here, from swirling it on downstream. Three trips were necessary to take the crowd across.

Without the Roebucks here to lead them the Beedle brothers, Jed and Lem, had throughout the day shown more initiative than the rest, had without declaring it assumed positions as Bentley's lieutenants. In their early twenties, they were younger than most of these people, but the men appeared to accept them and the arrangement was a help to Bentley. He crossed with the first contingent and delegated the Beedles to supervise the other two, warning them to look sharp. With the force divided, Boss Herbert could attack from the screen of buildings.

Bentley dismounted the six men with him on the ferry to use their horses as shields. Laying their rifles across their saddles they kept a close watch on the windows and doors but saw no movement. They walked the animals off the raft and waited in the lee of the sharp bank until the final trip was made.

It was hot in the canyon bottom. The little town baked under the midday sun and there was no one on the street. Four ponies drooped, stomped, switched their tails at flies at the rail before the board and batten hotel that housed the only saloon, but Boss Herbert's big grey was not among them.

Cal Bentley mounted his troop and rode in with caution. In the shade of the livery runway the hostler slept in a chair, his hat pulled over his eyes. They saw no one else. Bentley stopped beside the ponies, tossed his reins to Clem Beedle, said a curt, "Wait", and stepped down, crossed the board walk and walked into the saloon.

There were several men inside. One, very tall, in a pink shirt and black celluloid sleeve guards, leaned with his elbows on the bar talking across it to two loafers who nursed steins of beer. He nodded idly as Cal came forward.

"Hi, Bentley, what brings you down our way?"

Cal Bentley's voice was short, tight. "Boss Herbert. Seen him?"

"Yeah, he rode in late last night, had a couple of people with him."

"Still in town?"

"Nope." The bar man's eyes showed a lively curiosity. "They laid over an hour or so then lit out south. Boss was hunting his crew."

"Had they been by here?"

"Sure were, a couple of hours ahead of Herbert, but they didn't stay. Stopped for a drink was all. I thought it was funny as hell. What you want him for?"

"I want all three of them. For murder."

All the attention in the room snapped to Bentley and the bar man gasped.

"Boss Herbert?"

"That's right."

"Where's Brandy Ives?"

"Brandy's not sheriff any more. I am."

The bar man whistled, low, incredulous. "You're throwing news around pretty fast. What the hell is going on up at the Crossing?"

Cal Bentley was impatient to be riding but he wanted to leave a warning here, wanted to establish the courage of the settlers, spread the word that only they were willing to rise against the man who had for so long ruled this country by brute force. He made the story short and clear, and at the end of it a man down the bar growled.

"That explains the bastards. Cal, the damn Box H broke into my hardware store. I was sleeping in the back room and they rousted me out, threw down on me with one of my own guns and cleaned out every rifle and short gun and all the ammunition I had in the place. So they're armed again. I'd walk careful if I were you."

"Intend to. Thanks for the information, Pinky."

Cal Bentley turned down an invitation to have a drink and went out to the mountain men. They were dismounted, resting their animals, watching the street

84

with rifles loosely held but ready, an eagerness for action in their manner.

"They aren't here," he told them. "They all rode south, the crew over an hour ahead of Herbert's party. They have five or six hours start on us, and they took all the guns from the hardware store."

Lem Beedle yanked his reins free from the tie rail with a high call. "What are we waiting for? Let's go get them."

There was a scramble for saddles, an urgency to take up the chase that drew an order from Bentley.

"I set the pace, you follow it. Don't wear your horses out before we come up with them. You'll need something left in them then."

All through the sweltering afternoon they rode steadily but without haste. Lem chose three men he told Bentley were good trackers and Cal put them at the head of the column to read the sign the trail carried. At first the prints of three horses overlaid the larger group, then there was a milling at what could be judged a noon stop. Here Herbert's party had come up with the crew and the groups merged. Two miles further they all veered off, crossed a shallow ford to the far bank. There, instead of turning north toward Snakeshead Valley, they swung east.

Cal Bentley needed no tracker to show him the direction. What he needed was a reason for it. He sat for minutes wondering where Herbert was headed. There was nothing to the east except the long southern arm of the Burning Land and the tortured trail across that, over the mountains to the outside. But there was only one way to find them, to keep going.

Within half a mile the character of the land changed abruptly. From the rising slope of grass along the river the edge of the badlands chopped the ground into ragged rocky shapes like a tempest tossed frozen sea. The trail writhed across gullies gouged out by past flash floods. The ground was so hard that the little rain that fell did not penetrate and heavy runoff filled the gullies and small sheer canyons in minutes. More than one rider had lost his life, trapped by such quick walls of water engulfing him.

The uncertainty of Herbert's destination kept nagging at Bentley as they worked deeper into the scourged country. Opportunities for ambush were everywhere here. The conviction came suddenly that this was Herbert's aim. The rancher was using himself and his crew as bait to tempt Bentley's troop far enough in here to be trapped and cut off. He called back the trackers and halted the file. Lem Beedle pushed his horse up to Bentley's side.

"You get wind of something up ahead?"

"If you were going to set an ambush could you find a better place than around here? I think we're heading into a trap. Don't know any other reason why Herbert would ride into the Burning Land."

Jed Beedle joined them and sat looking about him. "Burning Land, huh? It sure is that. Good for nothing and spooky to boot. Where does this trail end up?"

"Goes through here and over the high mountains, then down to the road out."

Lem eased himself in the saddle and studied Bentley intently. "Maybe they're running out, leaving the country. Might be Herbert's afraid you'll arrest him again and Allen won't be able to break him loose."

Jed spat. "Could be his crew got the fear thrown into them and he's trying to turn them around?"

Bentley considered, then said, "Both are possibilities, but it isn't like Herbert to turn tail. We'll play it on the safe side. Hold your people here and let me ride half a mile or so on. I'll be out of sight and if they're up there waiting they may think I'm alone. If you hear shooting, close in, but take care."

Jed gave him a twisting, ironic smile. "We been in feuds before and we're still here. Plus, we want to be around to watch that Herbert hang . . . Allen too."

Lem put out a hand to stop Bentley as Cal started ahead and said diffidently, as though he were afraid of wounding Bentley's pride, "Like Jed says, we know this kind of game. Why'nt you let me go?"

"Thanks." Cal forced a small smile to show he was not offended. "But this is my fight from the beginning. You'll get your chance if I run into them."

He kneed his horse forward slowly, trying to recall the contour of the ground beyond. It had been years since he had used this track and his memory of it was dim. He rode with full caution, easing around each bend to study the stretch within gun range ahead. He was entering an area where high ridges rose before him, piling on each other into mountains. Over the ages water had sluiced a downward passage, cut deep into the lower ridge leaving cliffs on either side, and the trail wound between these cliffs. Here was the place. If the Box H was lying in wait for him this is where it would be.

He edged his horse into sight, scanning the tops of the cliffs and the folding slopes above them. Sunlight winked, drew his eye and he saw movement, a man rising. He kicked the horse around, heard a rifle crack and drove behind the bend he had just left while echoes of the shot bounced between the rock walls, covering the sound of where the bullet hit.

He dropped out of the saddle, pulled the rifle from the boot and slapped the horse on the flank, sending it back the way he had come at a slow run. The mountain men would pick it up on their way in.

He crouched against the nose of the bend, hung his hat on his gun barrel and pushed it out from the rock face. A second shot spun the hat away but Bentley saw the distant muzzle flash. He dropped to his knee, brought his rifle up and squeezed away his shot.

A high scream reached him, then he saw the marksman straighten, drop his gun and pitch headlong down the cliff and sprawl unmoving on the trail.

Bentley stayed where he was, his eyes sweeping that part of the cliff and ridge within his range of vision until pounding hooves behind him made him turn and draw back from the bend. The Beedle brothers were in the lead, heads swiveling and rifles almost at their shoulders. They saw Bentley on his feet and each threw up an arm to stop the men at their backs. Lem flung off his horse, his eyes bright with relief.

"Ambush all right. Did you see anybody?"

"One, and got him." Bentley nodded toward the bend.

Lem lay down and put one eye quickly out of the shelter, saw the body and ducked back. There was no shot to tell he had been seen.

"We can't get at them from here, that's sure. Do you know another way?"

"We can go back, find a place where we can climb and get on top. From up there we can look down on them."

"Top of that mountain? That's a big climb and it will be dark before we could make it."

Bentley looked toward the sun, only half an hour above the horizon, and agreed. "Either of you have any ideas?"

Jed had his look around the corner and whistled a low note. "Some spot up there. If I was running their show I wouldn't want everybody to spend a night on that hill. I'd put a lookout on the cliff to warn me, then I'd make a camp at the bottom to block us if we came up."

"Me too," Lem said. "Why don't we wait here? We'll hear them if they come down and if they don't, there's no moon tonight. We can go in quiet and they aren't about to spot us."

Bentley felt a glow of appreciation. They did think in terms of mountain war and their solution was much more sensible than climbing the mountain. Furthermore the rest would help them all.

They picketed the horses and settled into a dry camp back along the trail where there were upthrusts of rock on a slope easy to climb, good shelter if Boss Herbert, alerted by the shooting, brought his crew down. And although there were no clouds anywhere they would be out of the reach of flood water if it did rain in the heights.

Within two hours it was black-velvet dark in the canyon bottom. The tops of the hills on the east still held a ghost of light but directly overhead the stars were bright, giving them direction. Bentley took three men with him to scout the trail. They could move more quietly than the whole band. In the lead, he had Jed Beedle, one of the trackers and a boy he intended to use as a messenger if they located the Herbert camp.

They passed the broken body and felt their way beyond it, unable to see keeping one hand against the cliff to guide themselves. Every sense aware, they listened for any sound to tell them the men they hunted were near. They heard nothing, no whisper except the scurry of night creatures. A mile above the faint odor of wood smoke came down on the draft. They closed together, touched each other to be sure each recognized the meaning of the scent, then went on.

The track climbed, then the ground dipped downward. At the bottom of that grade the area of sky over their heads widened out, defined by the black shape of the ridges against the mottle of stars. The bottom there was some four hundred feet wide. The acrid smell was stronger, indicating that the camp was near. Bentley put a foot down, skidded and fell, caught himself on one hand in damp soil. He pivoted to his knees and reached to stop the men behind him, pull each in turn to a crouch to feel the wetness. Remembering the spot he whispered a description of the tiny seep spring and the little oasis of grass it supported.

"This is where they are. Donny, go back and bring our people . . ."

"Hold on." It was the tracker, Lloyd Lund. "You, hear any horses? Smell them? I don't."

Jed Beedle's whisper was sour with disappointment. "You mean they pulled out or they ain't been here?"

"Let's find out," the boy said, and before they knew what he meant to do he struck a match to look for prints in the damp soil.

Bentley slapped it away and as the little flame arced to the ground a rifle fired from the rim on their left. Jed Beedle gasped a curse, that he was hit. Bentley caught Donny's arm, shook it and told him fiercely to go back for the troop, heard his running feet, then groped for Jed and found him sitting in the mud.

"Is it bad?"

"My leg, damn it."

"Lloyd, help me get him away from here, quick."

But the tracker was not there. A second later his muzzle flash bloomed from twenty feet away, then from a different spot. Both shots drew fire from above but Lloyd had distracted the attention of those on the rim from the immediate location of the spring.

Bentley helped Jed to his feet and with an arm around him supported him as Beedle hobbled back along the trail, around the nearest turn. Cal lowered him there, out of reach of the guns, then felt hurriedly along the rock face. He wanted a fissure that he could climb, to put himself on the ridge where he could divert Herbert's crew from the bowl. They were shooting systematically, searching the area with lead. Lloyd's gun was quiet now, whether by choice or because he had been hit, there was no way to tell.

But the face was too steep here. Racking his memory he finally thought of a hogback of solid rock that nosed down to the canyon floor, some way ahead, beyond the bowl. Moving carefully he hugged the wall beneath Herbert's guns, skirted the grassy meadow until he passed that, reached the rock slope and felt for hand and foot holds.

It was slow going. He did not hear Lem Beedle bring his crowd up until they began shooting at the heights, aiming he assumed at the flashes of fire on top. A night fight, he thought, was a waste of ammunition, but the mountain men had more experience with this kind of warfare than he. He hoped they knew what they were doing and would not let themselves be trapped.

Through the night the firing tapered off. Bentley climbed, found gullies he could not cross and had to backtrack to try other routes. Dawn had touched the peaks and light was filtering down the slopes when at last he made a final grade on his hands and knees, coming up on a knife-sharp crest of the highest ridge.

He sat there just below the top where he would not be silhouetted against the brightening sky and looked into the bowl. It was still dark there and muzzle flashes sparked on the far side, never twice from the same spot. He could not say whether all of his men were shooting or only a few, moving from place to place, conserving ammunition. He could look down the slope he was on and further up the canyon see other flashes from the guns on the cliff edge. The light grew until he made out a rock slide. The mountain men were shooting from behind a jumble of boulders there, and as he looked a Box H rider stood up behind the bush he was using as cover, wanting a clearer shot, and fired.

Bentley shot, caught the man in the back and saw the body cartwheel into the canyon. He did not wait to see it land but scrabbled across the ridge and lay flat, his head and shoulders above the crest hidden in the low brush. His shot brought the Box H around to face the new attack and bullets whipped against the slope where he had been, whining off as some ricocheted. He ducked, let the volley subside, looked again and saw figures changing their places. He hit a second man, then a third before their bullets came like hornets swarming toward him again.

Again he ducked to wait it out. The firing was more prolonged this time and sounded as if it were coming from a greater and greater distance. Then it stopped. He risked another look and this time saw the crew in a running retreat away from his position and toward the ridge top, already out of range of his gun. The mountain men were firing and Bentley saw two of the Box H fall before Herbert's crew put enough distance between themselves and the guns in the bowl to have reached safety.

Cal Bentley stood up and for the first time saw down the far side of his ridge. A large valley lay at the bottom, a valley he had not known was there, stretching bleak and broken, boulder strewn toward the northeast. Box H was crossing the crest and running, jumping down toward a bunch of horses picketed at the bottom.

He sent a shot after them, knowing they were too far off to hit, and watched helpless while they reached the animals, mounted and drove across the valley.

There was no way he could catch them. He could only descend to the bowl, pick up his people there and ride around the ridge to find Boss Herbert's trail.

Beside Jed Beedle's wounded leg his volunteers had lost one man dead. The leg was bound in a rag and the men were piling rocks on the new grave to prevent predators from getting to the body. Lem Beedle was angry in frustration that they had not hurt Box H more, and impatient to take up the hunt again.

Cal Bentley insisted that they sleep until noon, warning them that they had a long trail ahead. He was worried about food. They did not have provisions for a long search and he thought they might have to go back to Malcolm's Ferry before they tackled the big valley. But during the morning a doe with two fawns came down to the grass and Lem shot all three. Dressed out and the meat dried, supplemented with the cactus Bentley had seen over the ridge and water collected slowly from the tiny trickle of the seep spring, this could sustain them for a long while.

They set out in midafternoon, up the canyon until they found a deer trail that took them across the ridge, then they doubled back to cut Boss Herbert's tracks.

They found them just before dark and made a camp there. There was no use going on because they could not see hoof prints at night, they would have to wait for morning to continue following Box H.

By noon of the next day it was apparent that the crew was splitting into small groups, taking different ways, and the sign Lloyd Lund read suggested that all of them were riding hell bent out of the country.

Bentley chose the largest group to follow. That would most probably include Herbert and Garvey and Allen, taking four riders with them.

The trail was clear enough through the afternoon but by the next morning wind had come up and a dust storm blew across the land, obscuring everything, raising a cloud that blanked out the sky, blinded the men and made the horses fight to turn away from the blast. They could not ride against that flying grit, could only huddle in the lee of a gully and wait it out. It lasted half the day, and when it did subside even Lloyd Lund threw up his hands in defeat. All prints, all trails were obliterated under the new riffles of wind patterns in the sand.

CHAPTER
NINE

They had no choice except to return to the Crossing
and wait and watch. For Cal Bentley the turning back
was a sour prospect on more than the one score of
going in empty handed. As long as the county
commissioners thought there was any possibility of
Boss Herbert coming back they would remain
uncooperative and hostile.

Besides them there would be Beth Herbert's wrath to
face. He had no illusion that the rancher's daughter
would stand quietly by when he had wrecked the Box
H and arrested her father on the charge of murder.
That both he and Able Allen were now fugitives she
would also blame on him.

He dreaded facing Sally Roebuck most of all. There
was no denying that because of his actions she had lost
her father and possibly by now her uncle. His
homecoming was bound to be anything but victorious.

It was evening when he forded the Whitewater and
turned his troop down the main street of the Crossing.
The mountain men would stop by the hotel for a drink,
but although Bentley had offered them supper there
Lem and Jed Beedle refused for all of them. They were
anxious to get back to their families and cabins. Cal

released them from his service with the strong hope that he would not need to call on their help again.

As they dropped off at the hitch rail Bentley rode on to the livery where Huey Ellis was already on duty. The hostler popped out of his office, helping Bentley unsaddle and rub the horse down while he asked anxious questions.

"Did you find them? How many of them are dead?"

"A few of the crew." Bentley was short. "But none of those I want. They got away and I don't know where they went."

The barn man sucked in a breath of consternation.

"You mean Boss might be back any time?"

"Might, but it looked more like they were all splitting up and heading for the outside."

Ellis stood with his head cocked, thinking, then shaking it. "Running? Boss Herbert? That sure don't sound like him to me."

"No it doesn't." Bentley kept working on the horse, knowing it was as tired as he. "But Huey, the cards are all stacked against him and whatever else Boss is he is not a fool. He may have decided after he didn't trap me his game was lost and he had better try to recoup somewhere else. We'll see in time. We'll have to play it however it works out."

Ellis said nervously, "If he ever finds out it was me who tipped you where he'd gone . . ."

"He won't hear it from me and no one else knows unless you told it."

"Me? You think I'm damn fool enough to do a thing like that?"

Cal Bentley smiled a little at the insulted tone. "Then what are you worrying about?"

"Why . . . I didn't know but you might have mentioned it to some of them hillbillies riding with you."

"I didn't." Cal dug a dollar from his pocket and pressed it into the small man's hand. "Get yourself a bottle and relax. Anything happen in town while I was gone?" He wanted to know about Dude Harris and Seth Roebuck but he did not want to ask Ellis. He would wait until he got to the hotel for that word.

Huey tucked the dollar away, saying, "Your Colonel Ruggles blew in three days ago. Looks like he ought to be a governor with that white beard and mustache waxed stiff as a porcupine quill. Friendly though."

That at least was a relief. "How many men did he bring with him?"

"Six of them. They been riding around the valley looking things over. Who would they be?"

"The survey crew. They're here to lay out just where the dam goes."

"Uh-huh . . . Cal, I used to drive a scraper on the railroad . . . you think they'll pay better on that dam job than I'm making? Maybe I ought to quit and work over there?"

"I'll let you know when I hear, Huey. Good night."

Bentley was tired enough that he would prefer dropping on the hay in a stall here, but there were things that had to be done before he could rest. He had already turned toward the street when Ellis called after him.

"The Dude is sure going to be glad you're back. He was in here stewing where you were and cussing because he wasn't with you."

Bentley stopped and twisted his head. "Dude is out of bed?"

"Oh hell, he got up the day after you left. Morey had a fit but you know how bullheaded Dude can get."

"Thanks."

Bentley waved a hand and walked out, hurrying. If Dude was up and around there was one logical place to find him, and he was there, in the saloon sitting with Albert Floyd at the back table. The mountain men had already gone but the room was well filled with local people. Floyd was as usual too drunk to look up when Bentley reached the table. Dude Harris had a glass in one hand and swallowed the drink neat when he saw Bentley, then kicked out a chair for him.

"Time you showed up. Them squatters of yours was here near half an hour . . . where you been?"

Bentley sank into the chair and leaned back heavily. Dude was getting back to his normal cussedness and Bentley smiled his first genuine smile in many days.

"Cooling out my horse."

"Why'nt you let Huey do that? I want to hear what all happened that Boss got away from you. I only got that much from Lem Beedle."

Bentley knew he would get no information out of Harris and he quickly sketched the chase, the ambush and the trailing until the dust storm effectively stopped them, then he asked,

"What about things here? How is Seth Roebuck?"

Dude Harris grunted in reluctant admiration. "Was sitting up this morning. Doc Morey can't keep him down much longer."

"I'll go see him then." Bentley started to get to his feet but Dude put out a hand to stop him.

"If that girl will let you. I tried to sneak him a drink and she took my head off. The man who gets her will lead a dog's life. Just keep that in the front of your head."

"Me?" Bentley laughed aloud. "I know her less than a week and you've already got me marching down the aisle?"

Harris shook his head solemnly, sounding mournful. "Being so cocky is the way men get took. They're so sure they're safe, then some female comes along and scoops them up . . ."

The tone told Bentley that Dude was more than a little drunk and he had advice of his own for the rider. "You keep on like you're going you'll land back in bed seeing spiders. In the morning you ride on home where One Lung can sober you up."

"Sure, old One Lung must be awful lonesome up there . . ." Dude, now that Bentley was safely here, was having a reaction to the tension of waiting. He was growing sleepy, his head drooping. Bentley wanted to lift him out of the chair and steer him up to the room, but he knew that if he tried Dude would balk. If Cal left him alone the rider might stumble up the stairs on his own, or if he fell asleep here Cal could put him to bed after the other matters were attended to.

He got up quietly and walked through to the lobby. Doc Morey was in a chair there, reading a book, looking up as he caught Cal's movement, saying,

"Sorry you missed out on Boss. He's an old fox and this territory will never be easy as long as he's floating around loose. But I'm glad you're back. Between Dude and Seth like a pair of grizzlies with sore paws I'm worn out."

"I sympathize with you and I'm sending Dude home tomorrow. Shall I take Seth along?"

"He ought to stay in bed here a week more but I wouldn't bet a plugged nickel he will. If you want to see him go ahead but don't get him excited or wear him out."

Bentley nodded and went on to the upper hall. Lem Beedle had taken away the downstairs guards but two were still posted near Roebuck's door, watching him come, reserved and disappointed at the news of the failure they had already heard of. Bentley knocked lightly on Seth's door and Sally Roebuck's voice told him to come in. When he did the lamp was burning on the table beside the bed and an open book lay in the girl's lap. She looked at him without smiling, followed him with her eyes as he came to the bed.

Seth Roebuck lay flat, his face pale but his dark eyes fierce on Bentley and his voice held an angry rasp, saying before Bentley could speak,

"That damn Herbert crowd . . . Lem came and told us . . . As soon as that ring-tailed doctor lets me out of here I'm going after him. I'll run him down . . . I'll . . ."

Sally Roebuck was on her feet, catching her uncle's shoulders and pushing him back as he fought to sit up, urging him to calm down. After a minute he gave up the struggle because he had not the strength to continue it and dropped against the pillow with an angry groan.

"Go to sleep," the girl told him. "You can't run anybody down until you're well."

She took the lamp out of his reach, set it on the bureau and turned it out, beckoning Cal Bentley toward the door. He crossed the room quietly, hearing Roebuck's snore before he reached the hall, seeing Sally come out with him and close the door behind them. He motioned the girl to come with him and took her out of earshot of the guards, then faced her squarely, his shoulders rigid as if that could help him through the next minutes. He would rather face a firing squad. His torment was in his voice when he said,

"Sally, telling you I am sorry about your father and Seth is the most inadequate thing I can do. It was wholly my fault. I should not have left the two of them alone to watch at the jail. Able Allen is a coward. I knew it. I should have foreseen that he would try some trick. Instead I ignored him. Burning the Box H was all I thought about."

She looked at him steadily, the deep hurt in her eyes making her look like a wounded fawn watching the hunter who had brought it down.

"Yes, it was a mistake. But Cal, I brought them into the fight. We had all come so far to find a new home and peace. We had never known peace. I thought there was a chance here if Boss Herbert could be driven out. Now I don't believe there is. I've been listening to people talk in the lobby and nobody thinks the dam can be built, or if it is built that it will be there long. They don't know where Herbert is but they're sure he will come back, that he would blow up any dam he found here. Our men would fight if there was anyone to fight, but how do you fight a fear that has paralyzed this whole country?"

She had sat in this hotel listening to the dripping poison, watching her uncle, thinking about her father whose death had been for nothing.

"Let me take you to supper," Bentley said. "We haven't lost this war yet. Colonel Ruggles is here and work will start right away. We can talk about it at the table."

She drew away from him, backing away and raising a hand in protest. "No, Cal. I hope you win of course, but you're just as mule-headed as Herbert. I don't want to know you any better than I do. Besides . . ."

He did not hear her last word. Dude Harris's owlish warning flashed across his mind and brought an involuntary laugh. She gave him a startled, bitter glance and swung toward her room, her back stiff. Bentley caught her shoulder and held her when she tried to wrench free, saying hurriedly,

"Listen . . . Please . . . I wasn't laughing at you, Sally."

Facing away from him, her head high, her voice came cold. "What else is there you find funny?"

"Something Dude said. I'd rather not repeat it . . ." He stopped, flustered, knowing he was making the situation worse, and stepped around in front of her. "Please come downstairs. Seth is sleeping and you need to eat. I don't want to leave you alone up here."

She did not relent. She was as prickly as on that day they met when she had run him off his own land. "Why should I go anywhere with a man who laughs in my face and won't say why?"

He knew that he had to explain and felt the hot flush rise in his cheeks as he said awkwardly, "I saw Dude in the saloon just before I came up here. He's drunk and he has a spite against women. You'd stopped him from bringing whiskey to your uncle. I said I was coming to see Seth and he warned me against you . . . said to watch out or you'd sneak up and hog-tie me. It just hit me how he'd look if he'd heard you say you didn't want to know me any better."

Her eyes changed then and a wan smile touched her lips, but it was a smile and she let him take her arm, walk her down the stairs. Doc Morey was still in the lobby reading. He glanced up as they passed him, smiled at seeing them together, then went back to his book. The cluster of tables in the long dining room were all occupied except for one at the rear and Bentley held a chair for the girl.

There were no choices of food, you took what there was, American plan, a menu that seldom varied from beef, potatoes, tomatoes from a can and canned peaches. A waitress brought the heavy plates at once and Bentley, trying to open a conversation that was not so frought with tensions, said,

"This looks good to me. I can only eat venison for so long."

The girl wrinkled her nose. "I'd appreciate a piece of deer liver. Don't they ever serve anything but beef? Aren't there any fish in the river, for instance?"

"There are, trout." He found an easier smile. "But Ma Drewster who does the cooking doesn't like trout."

"She must not like pork either. We always had pigs back home."

Sally Roebuck was not relaxing but Bentley kept trying, speaking casually.

"There aren't many hogs raised around here and those that are are butchered in the fall, used in the winter. In summer there's no ice to keep the meat. But when Seth is better and I can get you back up our canyon you can have all the fish you want year round."

The girl picked at the food, ate a bite and swallowed it, her eyes on the plate, then she said in a low but distinct voice,

"There will be no year round for me in this country."

For a long moment the words did not make sense to Cal Bentley. When they did he shoved back in his chair as if he had been knocked there and sat saying nothing, waiting for her to confirm what she meant.

"I've been telling Uncle Seth what the town is saying," she went on. "He wants to stay long enough to hunt for Boss Herbert and kill him. But even if he doesn't find him he has decided to move on west. I'll go with him of course."

105

Bentley's mouth was too dry to speak. He tried but only choked. The thought shook him like a giant hand. As he had told Dude, he barely knew her, but the picture of his canyon without her there brought a sudden emptiness to him. He was still trying to catch his breath to make a dissuading argument when movement in the lobby doorway caught his attention.

He knew before he really looked that way who was there, knew the tall slender figure made to look taller by the high boot heels and the pale hair piled high on the head. Beth Herbert was coming in, had seen him and was walking at him with a regal, measured step.

Bentley groaned. He had known there must be a confrontation between them that must be ugly, but it should not come now. Sally Roebuck should not have to suffer it, but he saw no way to spare her. Trying to make the best of it he got to his feet as she reached the table and said in a controlled voice,

"Sally, this is Beth Herbert . . . Beth, Sally Roebuck. Whatever you have to say to me keep it for later, don't make a scene here."

The rancher's daughter ignored the seated girl, looking defiantly at Bentley and deliberately raised her voice. "So the heroic sheriff has come back with his tail between his legs. Cal Bentley, my father is twice the man you will ever be and you will not find him until he is ready to be found. When that time comes I would not like to be in your place."

Bentley stood silent, meeting her stormy eyes, hoping she had finished her tirade and would take herself away. Instead she turned her back on him and looked

106

scornfully down on the other girl, saying loud enough to be heard throughout the room,

"And you, you skinny little mountain trash, don't you know how you people are being used? I'll tell you. Mr. Bentley here set out to ruin my father not because of any altruistic irrigation district but out of sheer spite. I don't imagine he explained to you but from the time we were children he tagged around my heels like a puppy. Then a man I could respect came to town and I chose him. That is why Bentley initiated the law suit against the Box H. That is why he hunted up an old billy goat who thinks he can build a dam and why he hired your tribe to burn our ranch, pure vindictive jealousy. Understand that he is not going to get away with it. My father will win. He always wins. And you poor damn fools are going to get yourselves badly hurt if you all don't clear out of this country fast."

Leaving Sally Roebuck staring, Beth swung on one heel and strode imperiously out of the dining room. There was a snicker, a low wordless sound that agreed with the ranch girl's description of Bentley's motive. Sally Roebuck heard it, understood it, and a sickness filled her that it could be true. She stood up, saying faintly.

"I find that I am not hungry after all. Good night."

Before Bentley could stop her or say a word she was gone. She was barely through the door to the lobby when someone guffawed and as if a key had been turned a wave of laughter filled the crowded room.

Cal Bentley sat down and doggedly finished his supper, trying to calm himself. There was yet one more call he had to make that evening.

CHAPTER
TEN

Colonel Lyman Ruggles stood six feet four inches. His shoulders and chest were thick, his flat midriff beginning to thicken now, in his early fifties, his legs like tree stumps. He had served thirty years with the Corps of Engineers and early in that service he had first seen Snakeshead Valley and his dream was born.

He had noted the miles of winding flat meadow with the Whitewater rushing through it, the two headlands thrusting out from the walls of hills, as if they had once in ancient times been joined. The bench line above the valley had revealed itself to him as the level of a great lake that had been contained there before the river had flushed a channel through to breach the blocking saddle. The place cried out for a dam to be anchored in those headlands.

Through the years he had tried unsuccessfully to interest the army but the Indian hostilities and the westward push of settlers had been too pressing for such a civilian diversion. And in the meantime Boss Herbert had moved in and built his empire in the valley.

As his retirement time neared Ruggles had asked for and secured a permit for the dam from the federal government, had spearheaded the establishment of a water district, strengthened his political ties, and when the army released him he began to move. And ran head-on into Herbert.

He sat in his hotel room now with Cal Bentley, his shirt thrown aside, the white mat of curling hair as thick as fur covering his body. Each had a glass of whiskey at his elbow but neither was drinking, the charges of Ruggles' energy too strong as he questioned Bentley on the events of the past week to permit even so small a stray notion. When Bentley finished his report Ruggles threw both hands in the air and snorted.

"The man is an idiot. What does he think he can do to stop us?"

"He is not an idiot, Colonel. He considers himself a king and until now everybody has let him be one. I hope he has pulled out for good but I wouldn't give you odds on it."

"I'm not going to wait around on my backside to find out. Forget Herbert. How long will it take to pull down those fences?"

"Depends on how much help I have."

"Hire whatever you need and let's go to work."

"That brings up another point," Bentley said. "Those people I deputized . . . the commissioners are refusing to pay them. I'm stuck for their salaries unless you'll take them over."

"Certainly . . . certainly . . . and put on all the men you can from that shantytown. I want that valley cleared as fast as possible. Three dollars a day and I imagine your boys won't object to eating an occasional Box H steer."

"Maybe not." Bentley laughed. "But I heard a complaint earlier that some venison and fish would be a welcome change."

The Colonel reached for his glass and threw the drink down his throat. "So the kids can fish, but anybody old enough to hunt is old enough to work for me. Anything else you want?"

"Sleep. In the morning I'll begin rounding up a crew."

Bentley stood up, emptied his glass and left the room. He had intended staying at the hotel but the clerk had told him they were full so he started for the livery. Passing the door into the bar he caught a glimpse of Lem Beedle, elbows hitched on the counter, watching the lobby. When he saw Bentley he shoved away and went toward him.

Cal said in surprise, "I thought you'd gone up to camp."

"Started," the man said, "then Jed and I got thinking. You might want to get hold of us so I'd better stay in town to take the word up."

"Glad you did, Lem. I've got good news. You're all on the Colonel's payroll to work in the valley and in the morning I'll start recruiting across the river. Get some rest, then go tell the boys."

Beedle scratched at his nose thoughtfully. "I guess I'll go along and tell them now, I can sleep later." He gave Bentley a looping grin. "We got a dam to build."

They went out to the street together, Lem to mount his horse at the hitch rail, Bentley continuing on toward the livery. The sidewalk was full of people and Bentley caught snatches of conversations, all of them involved with the disappearance of Boss Herbert, the arrival of Colonel Ruggles and the survey crew, the chances that the Snakeshead project would really get under way. At the barn he slipped in through the rear door to avoid Huey Ellis and his inevitable questions, dropped on the loose hay of an empty stall without even pulling off his boots and was asleep at once.

He had the ability to relax completely and he waked early, rested and ready for a busy day. At the trough behind the barn he set Huey's cracked enamel pan under the pitcher pump, splashed it full and doused his face and head, shocking himself awake with the cold well water.

He needed a shave. He had not had one since the morning when he had pinned on the sheriff's badge and Boss Herbert had ridden him into the Burning Land, and the flat planes of his cheeks were covered with a curling beard. But that would still have to wait until evening when he planned to treat himself to both shave and bath at the barbershop.

Huey Ellis was asleep in his office and Bentley saddled without waking him and rode into the early light, across the ford to the shantytown that was just beginning to stir. He found one man outside a shack door, yawning and stretching, and told him Ruggles would hire anyone who would work and who had a horse, asked him to spread the word and call a meeting,

112

saying he would be back to tell them about the job in another hour. Then he went back to the hotel for breakfast.

Colonel Ruggles and his six surveyors were already in the dining room and Ruggles hailed Bentley to his table to make introductions, and made room for Cal at his side.

Fatigue, both physical and emotional, had made Cal's supper worse than tasteless, but the sight of the food these men were eating made him ravenous. He ate four eggs, a steak and potatoes while Ruggles made a drumfire of talk outlining the way he meant to conduct his operations.

The Colonel and the surveyors would establish a camp at the dam site to save the time of traveling back and forth from the Crossing. Their gear was already packed in three wagons and one of the six would double as cook. Ruggles said they would go out as soon as they finished eating. Bentley was to stay and organize the work crews, delegate some to rip out the fences and roll the barbwire into spools for the settlers to use after the dam was completed and the lake filled, and another contingent would be put to hazing the cattle out of the valley.

Just listening to the Colonel talk was exhausting. The surveyors' plates were barely emptied before Ruggles was on his feet, swallowing the last dregs of his coffee, leading the men at a lunging stride toward the street. Bentley sat on, rolling a cigarette unhurriedly to throw off the holdover tiredness that Ruggles' headlong way had thrust back upon him. He finished his smoke, plotting his day, then went up to the second floor and opened Dude Harris's door quietly.

Dude sprawled crossways of the bed, still in his clothes. The room reeked so strongly of whiskey fumes that Bentley thought a lighted match might explode it. An empty bottle lay on the worn rug in a wet stain, apparently fallen when Dude passed out, for he would never have knowingly wasted half an inch of liquor. Bentley stood over him listening to the harsh breathing, wondering if he should send for Morey, then decided against it. Dude had survived drunks before and at least he was lying down, his body mending.

Bentley backed out, eased the door shut, just as Sally Roebuck opened hers and stepped into the hall. She saw him and turned away but he caught her in three steps, stopping in front of her without touching her.

"I am sorry about Beth Herbert's behavior last night. She's going through a bad time too, but . . ."

She tried to walk around him, saying in a chilly tone, "It doesn't matter."

He moved to block her. "It matters very much. There wasn't a word of truth in her saying I am acting out of jealousy. I lost her to Able Allen, yes, and I'm grateful to him for that now. But it's the valley, the dam that are important. How is Seth this morning?"

"I am on my way to find out. If you will let me pass."

He turned at her side, walked with her to Roebuck's room, waited as she opened the door and started inside behind her. The girl closed the door firmly in his face.

He stood shaking in sudden fury, damning Beth Herbert and at the moment damning the feisty

114

mountain girl. He lifted a fist to pound on the panel, then did not. He did not have time for a quarrel now. Let her sulk until he could get back and make her listen to him. Angrily he stalked to the stairs and down, got on his horse and put it toward the river.

He had cooled off by the time he crossed the shallow water and rode up the bank into the ragged community of the settlers. There were more than twenty gathered, waiting for him. He stayed in his saddle where they could hear him better, began with Ruggles's offer of three dollars a day, then had to stop while they went through a spree of yelling at the bonus wage. When they quieted enough he raised his voice again, asking if any of them had ever worked with cattle. Two of them called that they had and he motioned them forward.

"You two split your company between you, you're in charge of moving the cattle out of Snakeshead Valley. One of you start at the south end, one at the north and work toward each other. Butcher what you want and drive the rest up the side canyons high enough that they won't drift back down to interfere with the dam construction. Ruggles wants to begin work on that by the end of the month. When you finish with the animals you can catch on at the dam."

There were questions and he was still answering them when Lem and Jed Beedle brought the mountain men down from his canyon. It was nicely timed so that he could get the whole force organized at once. He turned the job of the fences over to the Beedles.

"Roll the wire up in sections and leave it, then when the Colonel's wagons are finished hauling in supplies you can use them to move the spools up on the bench above the line the water will cover."

Someone Bentley did not know asked, "How long is it going to take the basin to fill?"

"Ruggles thinks the fall rains added to what the river brings in should raise it half way if we're lucky. Some years we have a regular flood in the mountains where the river rises, but other times there is little rain. The important thing is how quickly you can clear the valley and the dam can be built. We have to be ready for those rains when they come."

He left them then to gather their horses and tools, to separate into the individual groups and set out for the assigned tasks, four lines of riders with their camp wagons to wipe the last vestiges of Boss Herbert's empire out of the valley.

Going back to the Crossing, Bentley was surprised that it was already noon. The time spent with the men had gone fast. He rode directly to the courthouse, passing up a lunch. The wreckage of the jail had been cleared away but the jail wall was still open. Inside, the desk had been repaired enough to use and a new leg nailed on one chair. The shattered gun case was empty, whether the weapons had been salvaged by the county commissioners or appropriated by vandals or the cleanup men. He sat down at the desk to take stock of what else there was to do.

A shadow across the doorway drew his attention and he saw Brandy Ives standing just outside. Bentley nodded and Ives's face relaxed and he came into the

116

room as if he had been uncertain of his welcome. He looked from Bentley to the hole in the wall and back.

"Lucky you weren't sitting there when that stuff let go."

Bentley made no comment on that. "What's on your mind, Brandy?"

Ives coughed, embarrassed. "The commissioners were talking to me about they're not happy the way things are going."

"They want you back in this job?"

"Well," Ives took off his hat and twisted it in his hands, "sort of. You see, Cal, there's more to being sheriff than arresting drunks and chasing outlaws . . . such as collecting taxes. They're due next week and I bet you haven't even sent out the bills yet."

"I thought that was up to the county treasurer."

"Naw, the sheriff sends out the bills and makes the collection, then he turns the money over to the treasurer to pay the bills the commissioners turn in."

Bentley gave him a half smile. "Fine. You're my new deputy to collect taxes."

The man hesitated. Being deputy was not what he had in mind. Bentley said,

"How much did this job pay you before I took over?"

"Hundred a month and one percent of the taxes I collected."

"As my deputy you'll draw one hundred a month and one percent of the taxes."

Startled, Ives said, "What's that leave for you?"

"Nothing."

"Then what do you want to keep the job for?"

117

"If Boss Herbert shows up I want to be able to swear in enough deputies to handle him. Also, I want to be in a position to arrest anyone who interferes with Ruggles or any of the men building the dam."

Brandy Ives took a quick backward step as though he had been pushed and he said sharply, "You think there's any chance he will come back?"

"You know him as well as I do."

Ives swallowed, then said slowly, "That being the case maybe I don't want the job again."

"You can always quit. You did once. And I need you."

Brandy said suspiciously, "What makes you so all fired anxious to have me?"

"I've got too much to do to chase around making folks pay taxes they don't want to pay."

The ex-sheriff appeared to recall something the commissioners had instructed him to say and his manner hardened abruptly.

"Such as sending them damn farmers out to round up the Box H cattle? What right have you got to do that? It sounds to me like rustling."

Bentley tipped the chair back and gave the man a thin smile. "Does it, Brandy? Have you forgotten there's a court order directing Herbert to take down his fences and move his herd? He wouldn't obey it himself so I am acting under that order. Do you want to be deputy or not?"

"You got answers for everything." In spite of himself there was a note of admiration in Ives's voice. "Well . . . I guess you hired yourself a man."

118

Bentley let the chair drop back, yanked open the desk drawer that stuck since the explosion, found a badge and stood up to make a ceremony of pinning it on Ives's vest.

"You are in charge of any civil matters and any routine arrests. I don't want to be bothered unless you need help."

Ives growled, offended. "I ran this office a long time without help."

"And did a good job as long as you didn't cross Boss Herbert. First things you do are get a mason to rebuild that wall and find some furniture . . . find where the guns went and get them back. After that you're on your own."

"I got the guns home. Where do I find you if I want you?"

"At the ranch, at the construction camp, supervising the crews in the valley. I'll be moving around."

He watched Ives settle into the chair with the air of a man returning home, then left the building with one load removed from his shoulders. He had been concerned at how to manage the routine duties of the office and have time to help Ruggles speed the work of the dam. Brandy Ives was the best possible solution he could have found to that problem.

He went back to the hotel with two goals, to try to knock the chip off Sally Roebuck's shoulder, then to take Dude Harris home to the ranch, away from the saloon. Doc Morey saw him from his office window, yelled at him and hurried down the stairs and across the street, calling ahead.

"Where the devil you been all morning that I couldn't find you?"

Bentley laughed. "At the courthouse for the last hour. Where would you expect to find the sheriff? Why?"

Morey snorted, sounding disgusted. "Dude took off."

"Oh? For where?"

"The ranch I hope. He was still pretty drunk. Has enough whiskey in him it will take a week to get it out of his system, and he went out of here muttering about what he'd do when he caught up with Boss Herbert. They're neither one in any shape to go on the warpath."

"Neither . . . Is Seth gone too?"

The doctor nodded. "Weak as a kitten and roaring vengeance."

"Do you know where he went? Did he go alone?"

"The girl went with him, said she could keep him in hand but I doubt she's up to sitting on that old rooster. They went up to their camp in your canyon. Believe me, Cal, I am glad to be shut of those two patients."

CHAPTER
ELEVEN

Cal Bentley worried throughout the ride and relief gave him a physical reaction when he pulled into the ranch yard and saw Dude's horse in the corral. He rode around the house, swung down and hitched his mount to the post there, then went through the kitchen door. One Lung was scrubbing clothes in the iron sink, taking out a bad temper on them, grumbling when Bentley came in.

"Stay away all week. Nobody tell me where. Now Dude come home drunk, can't talk, pass right out. Bring me just empty bottle. What you bring?"

"Nothing to drink, One Lung. You know your stomach can't stand whiskey."

The Chinese grunted at him then gave him a rueful smile. "Rice wine better for it, okay, but got awful dry all time by self, betting you in trouble . . . Hey . . . What you wearing star for?"

Bentley held up a hand to stall the questions, went on to Dude Harris's door and looked in. The little rider was in bed, a shrunken, exhausted looking figure under the covers. They were tucked in under the mattress and Bentley knew that aggrieved as One Lung was he had wrestled the clothes off Dude and ministered to him like he would a child. Reassured as to that he turned back to the kitchen, saying,

"Thanks . . . When he wakes up he can tell you about the week. Make me a sandwich, will you?"

The Chinese clamped his fists on his lips and shook his head. "Very fine dinner ready very soon. You wait."

"No time, One Lung. Never mind, I'll get it."

He found cooked steak in the cold press, slapped a piece between two thick slices of bread and went out to the horse munching, conscious of the cook's annoyance and disapproval. He mounted again and rode up to the camp in the bowl above.

The dogs and children announced his coming and by the time he reached the cluster of wagons the women and youngsters were gathered outside wanting word of their men. He told them they were in the valley and would be staying there, working, that he would see that what food and supplies were needed here would be brought up, and then asked where Seth Roebuck was. The Roebuck wagon was pointed out and Bentley saw the figure lying in the shade under it, wrapped in blankets in spite of the heat.

"He couldn't get up the step," a woman said, "and he wouldn't take our help. He's too prideful."

Bentley rode to the wagon and dismounted, squatting to look closely at the mountain man. Roebuck was awake but his eyes were dull and when Bentley spoke to him his answer was a weak quaver. Yet it was a stubborn insistence that he would be all right. Proving him wrong he immediately lost consciousness.

122

Bentley stood up and asked a boy watching with wide eyes where Sally was, and when he pointed at the wagon box called her name.

The answer came back in exactly the waspish tone in which she had first ordered him out of the bowl. "What are you doing here?"

He spoke to the canvas cover. "You'd better come out and talk to me. Your uncle isn't good."

The flaps parted and the girl jumped down, crawled under the wagon and tested Roebuck's wrist, then laid it gently on his chest and stood up to face Bentley, her voice worried.

"The ride up here was too much. I tried to keep him from coming but he wouldn't listen."

"I'm going to take him back and I don't want an argument."

She gasped as if she thought he was crazy. "Like he is? How do you think he could ride?"

"In the wagon. Make up a bed and I'll drive you down."

Abruptly she nodded and swung to the boy. "Tim, go get Noel to help and bring in our team . . . Hurry now."

The boy ran, calling to another on his way to the makeshift corral where all the families' animals were penned, and by the time Sally had the bed ready and Bentley had eased Seth out from under they were back, bringing a pair of dray horses. It took the four of them to lift Roebuck and carry him into the wagon, the camp women crowding around to do what they could.

When the team was in its yokes and Bentley's horse tied on behind, Cal climbed to the high driver's seat, gave the girl a hand up over the off wheel and put the animals into a walk. Sally did not stay beside him but crawled into the bed where she could watch Seth.

It was a tedious drive. Cal Bentley had hoped to be able to talk to the girl but something in his own stubbornness would not let him call through the canvas to her and she did not come forward. Long after dark he brought the wagon up before the hotel and put his head through the flap to say they had arrived.

"I'll go round up some hands to carry him," he said shortly, "then I'll hunt up Morey."

"I don't need no carrying. I can walk myself." Seth Roebuck's voice was stronger, had lost the quaver, and Bentley heard him thrashing out of the blankets.

Cal shrugged, dropped down and went to the back to help if it was needed but the mountain man scrambled out alone, climbed the steps to the porch and then the stairs to the second floor. Bentley followed to catch him if he fell, then turned back as Roebuck made it through the room door. Passing the dining room door he had seen Morey eating a late supper and Cal headed that way.

Morey had been across the river helping a baby into the world and he listened to Bentley with a sigh of resignation, finished his meal quickly and went up to his returned patient. Bentley left to take the wagon and horses to the livery, drove up at the rear and walked into the runway for a lantern to show him what he was doing. Huey Ellis popped out of his office like a trapdoor spider, full of news, saying in a rush,

"He's back, Cal. Boss Herbert. He sent in for his girl right after dark."

Bentley, reaching for the lantern, whirled on the barn man. "He's in town? Now?"

"I didn't say that . . . I said he sent in for her. Lanny Norton come slipping up the alley and called me out there where he wouldn't be seen. He told me to go tell Miss Beth he was waiting for her by the corral. Told me to bring her and saddle up her horse."

"Did she come with you?"

"Not exactly. She was in the hotel lobby and when I gave her the message she said she'd have to pack a bag and sent me on to get the horse ready. I got back here Norton was gone. She came along pretty soon with a little bag she told me to hang on the saddle, then she give me a dollar and told me not to say anything to anybody, especially to you."

"Which you have just done."

"Well of course. You're the sheriff, ain't you? Besides, you been giving me dollars for a long time and this is the first nickel I ever had from any of the Herberts."

"Thanks. Did you see which way she went?"

"No I didn't. I held the horse while she got up, then I come back in the office and shut the door so she wouldn't think I was spying. And I was afraid to follow and look in case Norton was out in the dark watching to see I didn't."

Dutifully Bentley handed over another dollar and told the liveryman to unhitch the Roebuck team. He debated taking his horse and trying to find the trail of the girl and the Box H rider, but even if he picked up the tracks in the alley they would not tell him much. Whatever direction they took they could change to another outside of town and in the darkness there was no way to follow.

He unsaddled, farmed his horse into the corral and returned to the hotel for a much delayed supper. It was now nearly midnight and the dining room was empty, but he had barely sat down when Sally Roebuck came in. She hesitated when she saw him, then came directly to his table and sat down and said quietly,

"I'm glad you're still here. I was too worried before to thank you for bringing Uncle Seth to town. He's sleeping easily now."

Bentley opened his mouth to tell her Huey Ellis's news but the night waitress came from the kitchen, announcing,

"Nothing left but steak and eggs. How many you want?"

The girl ordered eggs only. Bentley chose both, waited until the waitress had left, then said in a low voice,

"Boss Herbert is back in the territory somewhere. He sent a rider in to get Beth. Where they are I don't know."

The girl thought it over. "That sounds like good news. Maybe he isn't back, maybe they're leaving the country for good. He would surely take his daughter."

"I hope. But where Herbert is concerned nothing is certain. We'll just have to watch."

As the days passed Sally's guess appeared more and more correct. There was no indication from any of the neighboring communities that any of the Box H people had been seen.

The work of the survey crew went steadily ahead. Ruggles's team ran their levels, first for the dam, then around the valley staking off the projected high water level. All of the fencing was down, rolled and moved up to sufficiently high ground. The valley was swept of cattle, the animals hazed into the tributary canyons and Bentley expected that the small ranchers whom Herbert had hounded were quietly running new brands over the Box H, taking their revenge.

Colonel Ruggles was jubilant at the progress being made. He had opened a hiring office in the Crossing, offering jobs to any of the townspeople who would take them and to the new emigrants still arriving.

Cal Bentley spent much of his time at the survey camp as it was moved, to stay within easy reach of a day's work, interested to see the lines stretch out, drawing a picture of the lake-to-be. He saw little of Ruggles who was off buying horses, hauling in scrapers, preparing to start the actual work of moving dirt for the earth fill dam. Why that construction had not yet begun Bentley did not know.

The stakes marched up to the head of Snakeshead Valley and began the turn. They were at the halfway mark on the night Ruggles surprised them by riding in an hour after the crew had finished their evening meal. The cook kicked up the fire, put the coffee pot back to heat and sliced meat into the frying pan. Ruggles had just returned from a trip to the state capital and had ridden out immediately to see how much had been done. Finding Bentley there was a dividend to him and he launched into an account of his trip, overflowing with enthusiasm, talking as he ate.

"We're ready to roll now, Cal." The big voice carried through the camp. "The thing that's been holding me up is money. The state bank kept jumping from one foot to the other, couldn't make up its mind whether or not it would finance the dam. I finally knocked their heads together, convinced them that as soon as the reservoir was filled and the people settled on the land the fees for irrigation would more than satisfy the interest and payments on the principal of the loan . . . Any trouble around here?"

"None." Bentley always felt that the breath was being pounded out of him by the rush of this man's words.

"No word of Herbert?"

"Not a sound. It must finally have gotten through to him that he had to give up. After all, if he could somehow come back tonight with a free hand it would take him years to put the Box H back together."

The Colonel grunted, a highly satisfied sound, tossed away the dregs of his coffee and stood up to stretch the saddle stiffness out of his body, the big frame a dark hulk between Bentley and the flames. The talk of Herbert sent a thought through Bentley that the man was an ideal target standing so and he said quickly,

"I don't mean to sound spooked but you're taking a risk, against that fi . . ."

128

A shot cut off his word. The whip crack of a heavy rifle. Ruggles threw out both hands, then clamped them against his wide chest, sagged partly around and dropped like a felled tree across the fire bed.

Bentley was up and running, grabbing one arm, yanking Ruggles out of the sparks that fountained up around him. He beat with his hands at the smoking shirt and the little rills of quick flame that ran through the white beard and hair. But the Colonel did not know. He was dead.

The survey crew came alive out of their initial numbing shock, pulling their guns, peering into the night, but there was no moon and the dark was heavy. They fired into it anyway, then the drum of a running horse told them the rifleman was escaping. They ran for their picketed animals, saddled feverishly, but before they could mount the sound of the hooves had faded.

Whoever the murderer was, he had followed Ruggles here, or had the camp been staked out and patiently watched? Bentley found no profit in speculation. He dropped his gun back in its holster, not really aware that he had drawn it, and stared at the body in disbelief. One second the man had been so alive, so vital, so driving in his plans for the future of the country, his commitment to the dam. Now he lay empty of everything. Would the project now die with him?

In bitter retrospect Cal Bentley understood that Boss Herbert had held this murder as his ace from the first. Nothing else could explain why ever since the courts had decided against him he had acted ready to take on the whole United States government. He had seen Ruggles and Ruggles alone as standing in the way of his re-claiming Snakeshead Valley. Now that the engineer was gone Herbert would undoubtedly move again to return here.

Bentley's jaw set. He would prevent that return if it was the last thing he did. He watched with a sense of removal from the present as the crew came slowly in to the fire and one after another stopped to look down in silence at the quiet giant. Then they turned to Bentley. Borden, the head surveyor, said in a dry voice,

"Now what happens?"

Bentley breathed deeply, ordering his thoughts to make one step at a time. "First we take the Colonel's body to the Crossing. Then notify his family."

"Hasn't got one. Told me once he hadn't anyone left."

"Who takes over the work here?"

"You've got me. The way I understood it, Ruggles was the water company. The permit for the dam was in his name and so was the permit to establish the irrigation district."

"Hell . . ." Frustration made Bentley explode. "The world doesn't stop because one man dies. There's another way. There has to be. We'll keep working. You go on running lines while I find out what to do."

Borden lifted and dropped his shoulders, turned his back and walked to the group standing aimlessly beyond the fire. Cal Bentley felt pushed, compelled to action. He stalked to the holding corral, brought out a team and yoked it to an empty wagon, then called for

130

help to lift the heavy body and lay it on the wagon floor. He was ready to climb to the seat when Borden stopped him.

"Before you go you ought to know . . . We've talked it over. There's no secret about the trouble over this valley, not hard to figure who had the Colonel shot . . ."

"No it is not." Bentley's voice was hard.

"So, frankly, the boys don't want to get shot too."

"What does that mean?"

"Means we're pulling out."

Cal Bentley could not really blame them. This was not their fight and they owed no loyalty to him, none to the country. They were hired hands and no more.

"Pack up then and go," he said. "I'll have to get someone else."

CHAPTER
TWELVE

Night paled and dawn drew a thin gray streak along the crest of the mountains when Cal Bentley's wagon rumbled into the Crossing. He stopped it before the hardware store. David Moss ran that and the undertaking parlor behind it and lived on the floor above.

Bentley's boots echoed in a hollow dirge as he climbed the outside stairway. His fist made a dull pounding on Moss's door. Those were the only sounds in the sleeping town, the sounds of death.

It was several minutes before Moss's cranky voice demanded what the hell was wanted. Bentley pounded again. He did not want to shout his news into the silent street. Then Moss cracked the door and put his head out. Bentley said,

"Colonel Ruggles was killed last night."

Moss pulled the door wide, showing his long night shirt and skinny legs below it, his eyes becoming bird bright.

"Accident?"

"No. Murder."

Moss continued standing there, saying nothing more, speculation holding him.

132

Bentley said, "He's in a wagon down below."

"Oh." Moss galvanized into action. "I'll get my pants on, be right down."

Bentley went down the stairs and shortly Moss clattered after him, trousers pulled up over the night shirt and untied shoes on his bare feet. He unlocked the door at the side of the building and helped to carry the body into the rear room and lay it on the long table. A half-built coffin rested on a pair of saw horses. Moss measured Ruggles's big frame with his eyes, looked at the coffin and shook his head.

"Won't do for him, sure. I'll get another made right away. He won't keep long in this weather."

Bentley nodded, knowing there were no facilities for embalming in the town. He turned to go. He did not feel like talking. Moss called after him.

"I suppose this means the end of the dam project?"

Without looking back Bentley said, "The dam will be built."

He went on to the street, drove the wagon on to the yard at the rear of the livery, then walked back to the hotel. It was still only five o'clock but early risers were in the dining room. Bentley got a cup of coffee and took it into the bar. There was no one there and he went around the counter, laced the cup liberally with whiskey, then sat down in the lonely room. Through the long night drive his legal mind had gone over and over the problem posed by Ruggles's death. He had only Borden's word that there were no heirs. He would have to investigate that first. If it were true, what was the status of the permits now? And where was Boss

Herbert? When would he make his next move? He sat now trying to think like Herbert, trying to read the brutal, unyielding mind. He did not hear the man come until Brandy Ives said from the doorway,

"They said in the dining room you were here. Understand your Colonel was shot dead."

Bentley's head snapped up. "Where did you hear that?"

"David Moss. I'm head of the cemetery trustees. He had to get my permission to dig a grave."

"Oh. All right." Bentley had had a quick suspicion that Ives had been told by a Herbert connection.

Ives was unpinning the deputy star from his vest, tossing it on the table, saying, "Boss Herbert, wasn't it?"

Bentley looked up bleakly. "There's no proof. I can't say for sure."

"I'm sure. I'll say goodbye while you can hear me." Ives went out to the lobby, then to the street.

Bentley sat very quiet, then with a vicious swing he swept up the star and flung it hard across the room. It rang on the flange of the brass cuspidor and dropped in. Bentley shoved up, walked woodenly to the bar and poured a second, straight shot of whiskey and stood, his hand tight around the glass, cooling himself down. Then walking deliberately, he went to the dining room and ordered a breakfast he was not certain he could eat.

He was chewing methodically on the steak when Sally Roebuck came down for a tray for Seth. As she came abreast of the table Bentley said in an undertone,

"Sit down here."

She stopped, saw the tight lines in his face and slowly sank into the opposite chair. Bentley's lips barely moved.

"A sniper killed Colonel Ruggles in the valley last night."

The knuckles of her hand where it rested on the table whitened. "It is starting all over again then."

"Yes."

"What will you do now?"

"The surveyors have pulled out. There are the horses, machinery, tools to be looked after. I'll take your men with me to do that first . . ."

"No." The word exploded from her.

"Why not?" His tone was startled. "They volunteered. They knew it meant a fight."

"When there was cause to believe they could win, make their new homes, yes. Without the dam they cannot settle here. Without Colonel Ruggles the dam cannot be built."

"It will be built. I am going to build it."

She shoved against the table, hard, leaning toward him, rigid. "How? What with? What money?" She sank back and said more calmly, "No, Cal Bentley, you're fooling yourself. You are being as stubborn as Boss Herbert and you do not have the power to back up what you say."

He told her flatly in a low monotone, "It takes stubbornness to do anything worthwhile. Listen to me please. As soon as I have the animals and equipment cared for I am going to the state capital and try to take

135

out permits for the dam and water company in my own name. If Ruggles could get them I should be able to. Then I'll go to the bank for financing. That's where Ruggles's money was coming from and a lot of it has already been spent. I think they won't want to simply eat that loss."

"Perhaps." She said it sadly. "But it will be too late for us. The summer is passing and you could not reorganize in time to do us any good. Cal, I am going to send a messenger to bring our men down, tell them all of this and let them make their own decision. Some of them may stay but others of us will leave. With Boss Herbert around here again I want to take my uncle away. He's sworn to avenge my father but he's an old man and he's hurt. He wouldn't stand a chance. Goodbye, Cal Bentley."

He watched her, brooding. She was right in one thing. The dam could not now be completed by the time the fall rains came. If they came in enough quantity. There would be no lake by the next spring. There could be no farming. And even if they had the Box H beef that alone could not feed the waiting settlers. If it took too long to get money for wages from the bank those people would starve. If they moved on now they might find some other place, some other work to sustain them. He reached for her hand and she let him take it.

"Do what you think you must, Sally. I am going to miss you more than I have ever missed anyone. Promise me one thing. When you get to wherever you go write to me, tell me where you are."

She was a long time answering. His eyes held hers until at last she said in a very small voice, "All right."

The waitress brought Seth Roebuck's tray and the girl got quickly to her feet, took it through the room and through the door without looking back.

Cal Bentley watched after her until she was out of sight. A deep sense of loss emptied him. There had been so much else to crowd him since he had met her that he had not realized how much he had come to love her. It was a far different emotion than he had felt for Beth Herbert. Beth had been a flame, excitement, careless gaiety, but she had grown into a spoiled and pampered woman. Sally Roebuck, small, slight as she was, had a solid strength that faced whatever came. She met challenge head-on in the same way Bentley himself did, and it was that quality of likeness that made her worth for him.

The urge filled him to go after her, tell her, ask her to stay with him, or to go with her anywhere. He could not. Dedicated to see the dam built, he must not leave. And staying to see it through meant an inevitable clash with Herbert. He could be killed. Facing this fight he had no right to ask anything of her.

He paid for his breakfast and left the hotel. By the time he was in his saddle he had decided to ride first to his ranch to tell Dude and One Lung he was going to the capital, to pick up clothes for the trip and to station Dude where he could watch the construction camp under the headlands just outside Snakeshead Valley. It could be seen from the top of the mountain that rose six thousand feet above Bentley's ranch and Harris would be in no danger up there even if Boss Herbert brought his full crew back to the valley. All he need do would be to keep out of sight. Then Bentley could take the canyon shortcut down and let the animals loose where graze and water would be available. The equipment would have to wait where it sat until he came back.

Dude and One Lung were sitting at the kitchen table over their third cups of coffee when Cal walked in. The Chinese rose to bring a cup for Cal as he sank tiredly into a chair. Dude looked at him critically.

"How long since you've been in bed?"

"Not last night. The Colonel was killed at the survey camp."

Dude had poured some of his fresh coffee into his saucer to cool it and had the saucer halfway to his mouth. He spilled it down his shirt front and swore.

"The hell . . . How?"

"Sniper. I'd say it's a safe bet one of Herbert's men. Ruggles is supposed not to have any heirs and Boss may have thought with him dead there'd be no one to carry on."

"Well, I guess he's right."

"No. I'm here."

Dude swore again, in a softer voice. "Don't do it."

"Why not?"

"Why should you? Damn it, nobody gives a hoot except them hillbillies and you don't owe them a thing."

"Just quit? Let Herbert have it all? I thought you wanted to get even with him."

"Oh, I'll do that. Just let him show someplace where I can pull down on him, but there ain't no sense in us taking on the whole world, is there?"

Dude Harris's words bit deeper than he knew. It was a terrific temptation to just get on his horse and ride away, leave Snakeshead Valley and all its problems and follow the Roebuck wagon. But something inside him would not let him quit. It had always been so, as long as he could remember. His father had told him when he was very young that anything worth doing was worth doing right, that the only reason the world had developed was because of people who believed in what they started enough to keep at it even if it meant their lives to complete it. He said heavily,

"You don't have to do anything. I do."

Dude Harris snorted, insulted, and his voice turned rough with a mix of hurt and anger. "I helped wean you, boy. It's a little late in the day for you to start telling me what I do or don't have to do. If you're going ahead why what the hell . . . I've fought for a lot less reason and loved it. Bring on the Box H and we'll bowl them down like tenpins. With them feuding mountain boys we'll give them a war."

"We don't have them now. They're leaving."

Dude Harris sputtered and looked blankly at One Lung. The Chinese looked back, the worry in his black eyes his only expression. They were silent, then Dude flung his hands in the air, flapping them in a single wave.

"The world is crazy and I'm crazy to live in it . . . Cal, I never told you, did I, that one time a party of gents had a rope around my neck. I figured I was a goner. Ever since I've knowed I'm living on borrowed time. And I wondered a lot why I bothered. So what the hell am I stewing about? When things pile up on me I go hide in a bottle and in the morning I wonder why. Reason I don't quit drink is if I did I'd know when I waked up I wouldn't feel any better later in the day . . . Let's get about it . . . Where do we start?"

"Ride up the mountain with me to a place I'll show you where you can keep an eye on the construction camp . . . Oh . . . The surveyors have pulled out."

"Them too. Guess I did hear that rats desert a sinking ship."

"Where did you hear it? You ever been within five hundred miles of an ocean?"

Dude wagged a finger in Bentley's face. "All boats don't sail on oceans. I've seen the Mississippi and they've got some pretty big tubs running out of St. Louis."

It was a relief to Bentley to laugh. No matter what you did or said you could never top Dude and just this small bit of exchange brought a relaxation to Cal.

"You know something," he said in a lighter tone, "we're beginning to take ourselves too seriously. It used to be we could play everything for laughs."

"Yeah, and you know when the change came? The day Able Allen came to town."

And that spoiled it again. "I'm pushing this dam to get back at Beth Herbert? It ought to please you to know she told me the same thing."

"Forget I said it."

140

Dude was embarrassed. It was one of the few times Cal had ever seen him out of countenance, but the rider had never liked the girl and had been jealous of Cal's interest in her. Bentley got to his feet feeling pressed for time, saying,

"Any time you're ready to ride . . ."

Dude reached for his hat and followed Bentley out, saddled and took the trail up the mountain. It led to a little bowl of rocks that Cal had named the Lookout, a place above the timberline where the thin soil did not even cover the basic rock and from it you could look for miles up the far side of Snakeshead Valley and across the range into the forbidding bleakness of the Burning Land.

It was not an easy trail and he had not used it for some years, but it brought back memories of his exploring it, pretending that there were hostile Indians on the valley floor and that he was a scout, watching them. The trace wound around the peak, cut through the last fringe of stunted, wind-twisted scrub trees and lifted to the stone-fenced bowl not half as big as the ranch kitchen.

From that nest Dude Harris looked down and swore viciously. Beside him, Bentley saw the construction camp, the cluster of sheds looking tiny, five miles away. Smoke billowed into the morning air and there were moving specks that would be horsemen. There were hostiles now indeed. Boss Herbert was burning the sheds, the wagons, the corral.

CHAPTER
THIRTEEN

Cal Bentley's first reaction was fury. All the equipment laboriously gathered by Colonel Ruggles would be destroyed or wrecked beyond repair and it was a safe bet the Box H would run off or kill the animals. He wished he was close enough to use his rifle, but it would take hours to make the descent and by then the damage would be complete, the vandals gone.

Or would they be gone? It flashed on Bentley that Herbert might then decide to wipe out the camp of the mountain people. If Sally Roebuck had sent her messenger, if the men had already gone down to the Crossing, the women and children would be alone without defense.

He swung his horse, saying across his shoulder, "Dude, if they come after the people in our canyon . . . their men are headed for the Crossing . . . tell you why later . . . Go bring them to the ranch . . . bring Sally and Seth in the wagon . . . or if Herbert takes his crew into town I don't want them trapped there."

He pushed his horse faster than he had ever dared on this trail with Dude close behind, calling,

"What about you?"

142

"I'll take the women to the ranch. We can hold it a long time since we're warned, but make tracks."

At the foot of the grade Dude spurred for the town on the river, Bentley crossed the ridge that separated his ranch from the foot of the mountain and drove up canyon, past his buildings and into the mountain top. Above the shouts of the children and the barking dogs he yelled to the women, waving them to him, seeing no men there. From the saddle he told them what he feared would happen. Shocked cries answered him.

"My foreman is on his way to the Crossing to bring your men back, and for your safety I'll take you all to my ranch."

A woman close to him asked, "Why is that safer than here?"

"My buildings are behind a narrow natural gate in the canyon, that's the only way in to them. The hills are too steep for a horse. Two people can hold the gate from up on the ridges, but if they can't the house is log, thick logs. It was built as a fort in the days when Indians were a threat. Now put your goods in your wagons while I help hitch the teams."

They scattered, running, the bigger boys toward the animals, the women and girls to throw their scant belongings into wagon beds without any attention to order. In less than an hour they were lined out down the rough track and in another hour they passed through the gate and Bentley directed the wagons to be placed to block it. He asked the boys which one could handle a rifle best and one sixteen-year-old was singled out. Skeet, they bragged, had won the turkey shoot two years in a row.

Bentley took him around the buildings and showed him a path up the west canyon wall and told him,

"Climb until you can see the trail coming up, hide there and watch. If anyone comes who isn't one of your people shoot over their heads."

The boy's face fell. "Why not kill them straight off?"

"To warn them off if you can, play for time. Just the first shot. If they keep coming, let them have it."

Skeet liked that better and with his long gun in one hand made a dancing, scrambling climb. Bentley left him and hurried to the kitchen where One Lung challenged him in shrill agitation at the invasion of women and children.

In spite of himself Bentley grinned at the Oriental's indignation and told him, "Here's your chance to show your stuff. Hospitality's the word. Make a lot of coffee and knock together enough food for thirty people. Can do?"

One Lung flounced around, not dignifying the question with an answer. Bentley went on through the house to the yard, confident that the Chinese would feed them all and well. No one had ever been turned away hungry from that kitchen. He paused long enough to warn a woman, ask her to spread the word that the kitchen was One Lung's domain and not to be entered except on invitation, then he moved quickly to the east canyon wall, a much harder climb than the west.

By the time he reached the rim and worked along that until he could look down on the trail below the canyon mouth he was out of breath, his muscles quivering in spasms. He sat down facing the edge, stretching his feet in front of him, resting his back against a boulder. With no sleep the night before and the long hours of riding, he felt bone weary, his body a heavy sagging weight.

The sun was hot and the rock reflected more heat. He nodded and fought the tendency. Time dragged. When he thought he must have been there a quarter of an hour his watch showed less than five minutes had passed. He yawned. Then he shoved to his feet trying to shake off the lethargy, and sat down again, his eyes fastening on the trail with hypnotic intensity.

His eyes closed. Sharp, staccato sound sprung them open a moment later, he thought. The shot, knife-like, slapped from wall to wall, echoed from one chain of hills to the next.

Wide awake at once he had his gun raised before he saw the horseman duck back around a shoulder on the trail below. He waited. He would have given a lot to have seen the rider, perhaps recognize him and be certain in his mind that it was a Box H man and not some vagrant wanderer happening onto the ranch. He stood up, trying to see over the shoulder but could not, and he continued there, expectant. There was no further movement, no further sound.

That there was something wrong about the angle of the sun occurred to him. He fished his watch from his pocket and in horror found he had been asleep for two hours.

A burst of firing rattled from farther down the canyon and thin, angry yells came up to Bentley. That would probably be Dude Harris and the men running into the Box H. It did not last. Bentley almost held his breath while he waited to learn the outcome, who would be first to come into sight around the shoulder. It was some minutes longer before a horse appeared, then Dude's familiar spidery figure riding it.

Bentley skidded and slipped down the way he had come and dropped into the ranch yard just after the line of men had ridden in through the natural gate. Dude and Lem Beedle were in the lead with a rider between them, wrists roped to the saddle horn, and as Bentley went toward them Dude grinned.

"Got here just in time, didn't we. We were just starting up the grade when the shot warned us . . . We'd have rode right into them without the warning. Instead we sneaked up and got this galoot. Lem buffaloed him before he got untracked."

"The others," Bentley was concerned. "They get away?"

"All but one and he won't go no place again."

"How many?"

"Don't know. They were in the timber and just drifted back deeper. We could hear them but couldn't spot anybody."

The men and women were gathering around the wagons, in particular the one where Sally Roebuck stood outside the bows, holding their conference. Bentley wanted to go and talk with her but that would have to wait. He leveled his rifle up at the prisoner and told him to get down. Dude leaned to untie the wrists and the man dismounted sullenly, showing plainly that he thought he was at the end of his road, looking about him like an animal trapped by a pack of hounds.

Watching him closely Bentley asked Dude, "Did you see Boss Herbert with them?" And when Harris shook his head he barked at the captive. "Was he with you?"

"Naw."

"Who led the crew?"

"Joe Garvey."

"Where is Herbert?"

The man shrugged. "I never seen him."

"You're not part of the old Box H?"

"Only been with them two weeks."

"Who hired you?"

"Garvey."

"How many has he recruited?"

"Dozen."

Bentley looked at Dude, not liking the sound of that. With so many new men Herbert could put twenty or twenty-five riders into the field. He said, "When you signed on did you know you were getting into a fight?"

He got another silent shrug.

"Where you from?"

"Here and there."

Bentley hit him. There was no warning. His fist cracked against the lantern jaw and the man dropped, lay in the grit glowering up at Bentley and Dude. Bentley said roughly,

"That's for being smart. When I ask a question I want an answer. We'll try again. Where were you recruited?"

"Great Falls."

"What were you doing before?" Bentley moved the muzzle of his gun to signal the man to get up.

He got slowly to his feet, rubbing at his jaw, his eyes flicking from one man to another. "Riding with Johnny Sykes."

The news was getting worse. Johnny Sykes had been a notorious train robber until he was caught and hanged half a year earlier and the men who had ridden with him were as tough as anyone in the country.

"Did all of Sykes's gang catch on with Herbert?"

"Five of us."

"Who are the rest of the new riders?"

"Drifters that liked the hundred a month and found Garvey pays."

Bentley asked again, "Where is Herbert now?"

"Garvey didn't say."

"Then who ordered the raid on the construction camp?"

"Garvey."

Garvey, Garvey, Garvey. The man sounded like a frog. Bentley had learned nothing of value except the quality of men Boss Herbert was gathering in and that had been predictable, and other matters were pressing, first what to do with the man.

Dude Harris read his mind and suggested they hang him to the closest tree. Bentley felt sure he deserved it after riding with Sykes but here in this yard with the mountain children watching was not the place. He ordered him bound and loaded into a wagon and turned to the next problem. With the Box H in the timber below they must prepare to stand a siege. He called Lem away from the conference to lay out a plan, post men on the mountain sides, others at the wagons blocking the gate, move the women and children indoors. But as he was talking the boy Skeet came skittering down from his lookout, waving and pointing. He had got a look at the Herbert crew in force, coming out of the trees and taking the tangent trace toward the upper bowl and the abandoned camp.

That changed everything. They should have time here to get the wagons moving on down out of the canyon and toward the Crossing. With luck they should make it to open ground before the Box H could burn out the crude shacks and come back to the ranch. He shouted the order, saw it register on the men, saw them scatter, climb to the seats and start the wheels rolling out through the gate, then Bentley ran to the house.

"Come on, One Lung, time to leave. We're going to the Crossing . . . and this place won't be here when we come back, so take anything you want to save."

The cook's eyes widened and his mouth made a round O, his feet made little up and down dancing steps of anger and his voice screeched.

"You going to let that Boss burn down your papa's house? Just run away?"

"No time to argue it, One Lung. There isn't enough food here to hold out for long. You want to see those women and kids either starved or butchered? Move it."

Swearing bitterly in a language Bentley thought the man must have forgotten, the Chinese scuttled for his quarters while Bentley ran on to his. There were few things he would take for himself, a change of clothes, the guns and ammunition, what little cash he kept here, and most importantly the large ruby ring that had been his father's pride. It took him ten minutes to gather it all and when he returned to the kitchen One Lung was waiting with a heavy portmanteau. From the way he bent to lift it Bentley knew the weight would be the burial money he had collected over the years.

Hurrying through the big living room, Bentley threw one last look around it. So much of his life would be left here. He could take with him only the crowding memories. Outside, Dude had One Lung's old white horse saddled. He helped to fasten the heavy bag to the horn, then the three of them mounted and rode after the wagons.

Because of those wagons they had to take the long route and their progress was agonizingly slow. Night came down before they reached the open bottom land and Bentley dropped back a quarter mile to listen behind them, but no thunder of running horses came to warn him the Box H was in pursuit.

Daylight was growing when the procession rolled into the shanty town. The rumble of the wagons brought the people there out of their shacks and holes and consternation spread in a wave as they learned of the evacuation of the canyon camp. Arguments rose as to whether these settlers too should leave the country.

Bentley came up with them and saw Sally Roebuck hurrying back to him and pulled up beside her.

"We are going to rest the teams here for the morning," she said. "Surely Boss Herbert isn't crazy enough to come and try to massacre all of us but if he does there are enough of us together now to fight him off. We'll leave this afternoon."

One Lung and Dude had stopped to wait for Bentley and Dude growled at the girl.

"You could all lick him if you'd stay and fight."

"No, Dude, she's right," Cal told him. "If there's no work they can't stay. Sally, where are you going? Have you decided?"

"Our people are going to California. Are you still going to the capital?"

"I am. If I'm successful there will you come back?"

"Not if Boss Herbert is still able to stop the work."

Bentley had an idea and said on impulse, "Would you take One Lung along with you? He's the best cook in the West and I don't want to leave him here while I'm gone. I'll send for him when I can."

"Of course." She smiled at the Chinese. "He'll be welcome. You'll come, One Lung?"

For a moment the old cook looked at Bentley as if he were being deserted, then his eyes turned sly and he grinned.

"Get chance to see San Francisco maybe. Find concubine to bring back like long time ago. Sure, I go."

Dude Harris squinted at him and snorted. "You really got an idea there, you old coot, and if Cal and I had half sense we'd trot right along with you."

"Go ahead," Bentley told him. "Nothing says you have to stay here."

"Nothing but a blockheaded mule I raised from a pup. You ain't getting rid of me that way. But we got another little chore to do before we start for that capital. When do we string up that gunslinger in the wagon?"

"We don't. He didn't do us any harm . . . He even did us a favor, showing up so Skeet could warn us. Sally, will you tell Lem to take him in your train . . . a hundred miles or so, and turn him loose."

She nodded and extended a slender hand. "We will . . . I wish you luck, Cal."

He took the hand, then dropped it and turned his horse. If he had held it a moment longer he would have blurted out the words he had no right to say. Quickly, before he could change his mind, he spurred the horse and drove it toward the ford, choking on the thought that he might never see her again.

CHAPTER
FOURTEEN

Cal Bentley slept through most of the stage ride. The town was not only the capital, it was the largest settlement in the state. The dome that dominated it was sheet gold, symbol of the pride that the state was one of the largest producers of the yellow metal in the country.

Bentley was familiar with the streets. His law practice had brought him here time and again, but it was Dude Harris's first visit and he gaped through the coach window at the big shape that gleamed like a rising harvest moon, at the long rows of tall brick buildings that faced each other across the dust ribbon of Larimer Street.

The Windsor Hotel where they stopped was five stories high, built of Castle Rock limestone, the interior decorated in gilt, silk paneling and plush, polished wood. Dude nearly broke his neck looking up as they walked through the rotunda where the ceiling was twenty feet up. Bentley held his arm to steer him toward the desk where he registered, then on to the elevator that lifted them to the top floor. From the window the foreman stared down into the street, then backed away from the precipice, whistling.

"This must be the tallest building in the world . . . it must cost a pretty penny to stay here."

"Five dollars a day," Bentley told him.

Dude spun around, aghast. "What are we doing here?"

Bentley began stripping off his stained and sweated clothes for a much-needed wash in the ornate basin, talking as he dropped them.

"I am going to try to borrow a lot of money from the Brown Brothers' bank. If I stayed at the Apollo or some other cheaper hotel they wouldn't even listen to me, but if they know I am at the Windsor they'll think I'm somebody important."

"I hope it don't take you long."

"We'll be here awhile, there's a good deal to do. I have to see the federal land office about getting the permits, and we'll have to hire a crew. I need thirty good fighting men to handle Herbert and then protect the surveyors and dam gangs from interference. That's your job, finding the men. You can start looking today."

The foreman moved around the room, testing the mattress, fingering the upholstered chairs, saying over his shoulder,

"Got the cart before the horse, haven't you? What do you do with a crew if the rest don't pan out?"

Bentley poured water in the bowl and shivered when he rubbed it over his body. It was chilly at this altitude after the blazing heat at the valley, but both the cool air and the water were more than welcome. He spoke through the cloth as he scrubbed his face.

154

"I'd rather gamble and have them ready than sit around later while you find them. I want to get home as soon as possible."

"All right if you say so, but where do I look?"

"The saloons and billiard parlors . . . that's what they call gambling houses here. You might talk to some of the madams along Holladay Street, they're apt to know the kind we want and can steer you to them."

"Well now," Dude sounded suddenly cheerful, "this is one job I'm going to like. I always heard the girls in Denver were something special . . ."

"And don't get drunk. Dude, the last thing I want is you to get yourself killed."

"Don't you worry none, I ain't letting nothing happen to me until I can settle the score with Boss Herbert. I'll stay sober as a judge. See you later."

Dude went out jauntily, whistling, to explore this intriguing town while Bentley put on the fresh clothes.

He left off the holster and belt he had worn coming in, planning to stop in a gun shop and buy a smaller weapon that would not be so noticeable, then he went down to the barbershop and luxuriated in a shave and haircut.

Ready now to tackle the land office, he walked to it and asked to see the manager, presenting his card. The clerk looked him over, took note of the neat business suit, the air of assurance, and asked him to wait. He disappeared into the inner office and a moment later came out and held open the gate between the waiting room and working area.

Bentley walked through that and into the office where a stout, bald man sat at a roll-top desk holding the card.

"Yes, Mr. Bentley?" The tone was neutral, reserved.

"I come from the Crossing, which is north of here . . ."

"I know where it is," the man said testily.

"I'm glad to hear it." Bentley kept the edge of temper out of his voice. "As you see, I am an attorney, and also I am acting sheriff of Snakeshead County."

The brown eyes that had been dull with disinterest came alive and the tone eased. "Isn't that where Colonel Ruggles is building a dam?"

"He was until a few days ago. He was murdered."

The manager straightened, looking shocked. "The Colonel murdered? By whom?"

"I can't prove it but I'm certain he was ordered killed by the man who ranched for years in Snakeshead Valley." Bentley sat down without being asked. "I don't believe I caught your name."

"Clark. William Clark." The man waved it aside as unimportant. "Do you know why he would do such a thing?"

"Because Boss Herbert lost a court case. He was ordered out of the valley so it could be flooded. He thought if Ruggles was dead the dam would not be continued."

"That's a very serious charge."

"Anyone in those parts who dared to talk would make it without hesitation."

156

"But . . . But what would Herbert think he could gain?"

"He's trying to hold onto the ranch in spite of the order. Is the land office prepared to send in men to throw him off?"

"Mr. Bentley, we do not have any personnel to do that. It is up to the local law enforcement agencies . . ."

"Which do not exist."

"You just said you are acting sheriff."

"I am. Because the man who held the job for years was afraid to go against Herbert. Mr. Clark, I deputized a group of men from Tennessee who had come to take up land and work on the dam. We arrested Herbert and his foreman and jailed them, then we went to burn the ranch. While we were out of town the banker, who is engaged to Herbert's daughter, dynamited the jail and freed the prisoners. The leader of the Tennessee men was killed and his brother badly wounded."

The man made agitated gestures, moving articles on the desk around aimlessly. "How can such things happen today? There must be some law capable of dealing with this."

"Tell that to the governor, to the legislature. Herbert owns most of the legislature and the governor would not have been elected without Herbert's support. Do you think I could get help from them?"

"Well . . . Well . . . What do you want from me? I have asked for federal marshals before but Washington has turned me down consistently."

Bentley laid a hand on the desk, leaning forward to command the man's attention, and said deliberately, "I want you to reissue the permit to build the dam to me. According to my information Ruggles left no heirs and even if he did I doubt they could build that dam against Herbert's opposition. I want the irrigation district under my administration so I can settle people on the land, farmers who can make that country bloom. And I want the land office to send us emigrants. We will have room for at least a thousand families when the reservoir is established."

Clark had been drawing little gasps as Bentley counted off his requests and only the last brought a sympathetic reaction.

"I know the country," he said. "It could be very productive. But there are questions to be answered before I could give you approval. In Colonel Ruggles's case there was no delay, but you'll pardon me if I say you are something of an unknown risk. I do not know that you could raise the money. I don't know that you wouldn't use the project to sell stock and make a swindle of it . . ."

Bluntly Bentley told him, "You don't. Although I know a lot of people in Denver and my record as attorney for Ruggles in the court hearings is on record. So tell me this, if the Brown Brothers will underwrite the construction can I count on your office for the permits?"

William Clark was startled. He studied the stranger, young, with a sense of drive about him, and abruptly he nodded. "If their bank will back you, Mr. Bentley, yes."

Cal Bentley offered a hand across the desk and Clark shook it, then Bentley stood up. He had taken the first round but the fight was a long way from won. He was moving into an area that was totally unfamiliar to him.

It was too late to approach the bank that day. He went back to the hotel, waited until a nobly sober Dude came in, then celebrated his first success by taking Harris to supper at the Apollo Hall on Larimer between D and E Streets.

Dude was awed again by the trappings but the subservience of the waiters disgusted him and the cuisine he found could not compete with One Lung's dishes. Bentley told him how it had gone at the land office and was disappointed that the Dude saw the victory with more caution than conviction, then Cal asked him what he had found out about a crew. On that subject Harris was excited.

"Son, this is some town all right and I looked in on a lot of it. I met a gal named Mattie Silks, runs a parlor house called the House of Mirrors and it is some class. Wait until you see it. We're supposed to go over tonight and meet a man she's got coming to talk to you. Name of Gordon."

"She tell you anything about him?"

"Says he's a ring-tailed one-man war. She knew him in Leadville. From the stories she told me he had that camp on a lead rope with a ring in its nose. And she says he can get us all the hardcases we need. She wants fifty bucks if we make a deal."

"Good day's work, Dude. I think the trip was worth it."

He was not happy to have to use this type of man but there was no hope of handling Boss Herbert with

159

ordinary riders. He needed a crew to match the Box H with its influx of toughs from the Sykes gang.

He knew Mattie Silks by reputation though he had never been in her place. He had stayed clear of all the Holladay Street houses. Outside of the Barbary Coast this was said to be the most depraved four blocks in the country. Here the pimps, called Macs in local slang, gambled, fought and stole in the cheap bars that thrived between the billiard parlors and cribs that jostled each other for room, without interference. Of all the western cities Denver was noted for the most crooked police department, the most venal sheriff's office and the greatest number of con artists crowded into one locality.

Bentley kept his hand on the new little gun in his pocket as they walked the gamut of the street to the House of Mirrors. A colored woman opened the door, said good evening and ushered them into the parlor where the walls were covered with mirrors that reflected the lamplight again and again. They also reflected the bevy of girls seated about the room watching them speculatively but saying nothing. It was early for business and Mattie Silks ran her house with a tight rein, demanding that her "young ladies" behave as such except in the privacy of their rooms.

Alerted by the maid, the Madam appeared, assured herself who her callers were and invited them into her own apartment. She was stocky rather than fat, her face round with a suggestion of double chin and she wore her blonde hair in bangs, parted in the center. She wore a rather austere dark jersey dress with an over-shirt of pleated white lace. When Dude introduced Cal Bentley her manner was brisk and businesslike. On the walk down the short hall she said over her shoulder,

"Gordon isn't here yet but he's due any minute. Can I offer you coffee or a drink?"

"Coffee," Bentley said.

She took them through her door, pressed a bell inside it and when the colored woman answered Mattie asked her to bring two cups, and motioned the men to chairs. When the cups came and Bentley tasted his he found it laced with brandy and watched Dude's pleased reaction.

Gordon arrived within minutes, a man as big as Bentley with a lean, savage face behind a flowing yellow mustache and pale blue eyes with no more warmth than polar ice.

"Come in, Frank," Mattie said crisply. "Meet Calvin Bentley and his foreman, Dude Harris. I'll leave you to your talk now. Carrie will bring you a drink."

She went out and closed the door, plainly not wanting to know whatever arrangements would be made. If a bargain was struck she would be paid and that was her only interest. Any further knowledge could lead to trouble and she wanted no part of that.

Frank Gordon had not offered a handshake. He stood looking Bentley over, ignoring Harris, until the maid brought a glass and bottle and left, then with those in his hands he crossed to sink onto a chair at the far side of the room. Something in the way he moved reminded Bentley of a mountain lion he had once watched as it crept along a ridge, closing in on an unsuspecting calf. Even his tawny coloring added to the illusion. There was an unmistakenly deadly quality about the man. He filled the glass while he said in a flat, empty voice,

"What's your deal, Bentley?"

Cal told him the background of why he wanted fighting men and finished, "I want men who can protect the people I'll have working there."

"You want this Herbert killed."

"I am not hiring a murderer. If he attacks and is killed in a fight, all right, but don't go looking for him. You will all be sworn in as special deputies. You will be a legal force."

"What's it pay?"

"Can you find thirty men?"

"Easy. If the price is right."

"The men get a hundred a month and found. You draw two hundred."

There was no change in the chill face. Gordon stood up, threw down a second drink, set bottle and glass on the table before he spoke.

"You bought a crew. How do I get hold of you tomorrow?"

"I'm at the Windsor."

Gordon walked to the door and out without another word. Bentley gave him time to get clear of the house before he and Dude went back to the parlor. Mattie Silks joined them there and escorted them to the door where Bentley counted fifty dollars into her hand, thanked her, then they went on to the street. They walked a block in silence before Dude Harris muttered,

"I hope you know where all that money is coming from."

"I do." Bentley's smile was thin enough to match Frank Gordon's. "It's coming from the Brown Brothers' bank."

CHAPTER
FIFTEEN

In the morning Cal Bentley was at the bank five minutes after the grilled doors had been opened. The institution, one of the first in the infant city, had begun as a private mint, turning the miners' gold into coin to simplify doing business in the mountain state. Bentley asked to see either of the brothers and was ushered into a large ornate office, heavily furnished with two desks, one brother at each of them.

They were polite as he told his story but aloof and disinterested. Bentley, having won the land office approval and found the core of a crew as hard as anyone Boss Herbert had, felt the whole great project slipping away from him as he faced the men on whom everything else rested. Talking to each in turn he tried desperately to paint the picture for them of what the vast area below the dam could become, what it would mean to so many people, to the economy of the state, and had for his pains a quizzical question from Morton, the elder Brown, asking as if he were some innocent schoolboy,

"What made you think we would advance money to you, Mr. Bentley? We don't know anything about you."

Wholly angry at the reception Cal threw caution and reason away and said bluntly, "Mr. Brown, you don't have much choice."

The brothers looked at each other, eyebrows going up in disapproval at such an ultimatum delivered to so august a house by a young man offering nothing but dreams as collateral. Morton made a steeple of his fingers and said with quick impatience.

"I am afraid I do not understand what you mean by that rash assumption. Please explain yourself."

"You advanced money to Colonel Ruggles for his preliminary work."

"Ten thousand dollars, yes, which makes us doubly unlikely to throw more money into a failed project."

Bentley turned caustic. With everything to lose if he could not jar these people out of complacency he snapped,

"So you intend to sit on your hands and lose that ten thousand, make no attempt at all to recover any of it?"

The second brother said, equally sharp, "Perhaps you know the banking business well enough to tell us how we can recover?"

That was a wedge and Bentley drove into it recklessly. "I will assume the advance to Ruggles if you will give me the loan for the dam. Ruggles estimated he would need one hundred and fifty thousand for completion. He also projected that the Snakeshead reservoir could supply irrigation water for a thousand farmers. The water district should pay off all loans within ten years.

"Now . . . The land office will give me the permits in my name as soon as they are assured I can finance the dam. I will do this, incorporate the water company and issue bonds in the amount of two hundred thousand, to cover extra labor. You people underwrite those bonds, either hold them yourselves or sell them. Then I will issue water company stock and turn over half of that stock to you. That's a good deal more than mere recovery."

He held his breath while they studied him. There was a change in the atmosphere. They appeared to be able to communicate with each other without words, then Mort said cautiously as if he were a fish nudging a bait,

"This Herbert person . . . I would think he would attack you the same as he did the Colonel."

"I intend to see that he doesn't kill me. I'm hiring thirty special deputies who are quite capable of standing Herbert off. With his cattle gone he has no income. When he learns that my fighters are at least the equal of his I think it will finally get it through his head that he has to give in and leave."

"Those hardcases, you can't trust any of them."

"I am paying them premium wages, much more than they could get anywhere else. Mattie Silks recommended their leader and I understand not many people along Holladay Street like to cross Mattie."

It was a lucky shot. Both brothers laughed and the tension in the room loosened. Mort said more easily,

"Well, we'll talk it over and let you know tomorrow."

"Tomorrow," Bentley pressed, "is too late. I have to hire my deputies this afternoon."

They consulted wordlessly again. It was obvious they did not like being hurried, but in his legal practice Bentley had learned that crowding a gambler more often than not would make him take a plunge that he would not if he were given too much time. And these men were gamblers, playing at very high stakes.

Morton pursed his lips, then said hastily, "Very well. We can reach you at the Windsor?"

"I'll wait for your message," Bentley said and stood up with deliberate confidence. He walked out briskly but took away with him a haunting doubt that he had sold the brothers.

He found Dude in the Windsor bar hunched over a beer, relieved that he was still sober, and sank onto a stool at the foreman's side, drained of energy.

Harris saw him in the mirror and sounded anxious. "You get the money?"

"I don't know. They'll tell me later."

"When?"

"I don't know that."

"What are you going to tell Gordon?"

"Stall him, I guess."

But Gordon had not appeared when an hour later a clerk came from the bank requesting that Bentley go back with him. The brothers received him immediately, this time with smiles. They already had an agreement drawn up. They would take care of issuing the bonds and he and the bank would share equally in the water company. It took a surprisingly little time before the money was credited to a special account and Bentley left the building with the first hurdles crossed.

Now all he had to do was give Frank Gordon a go-ahead, find surveyors, find laborers, buy equipment and horses to replace those destroyed by the Box H, and return to the Crossing.

Four days later his entourage lined out. Seven wagons loaded with supplies and tools, twenty-five teams for as many scrapers, a survey party of four, a nucleus of workmen, a remuda of extra horses for the deputies.

There was nothing to inspire confidence in the guards' appearance. They looked exactly what they were, outlaws, bummers from the slums of Denver, men who had killed and would again for as little as a silver dollar. Under his breath Dude Harris called them range trash, but Bentley needed guns and this crowd certainly could handle guns.

It was late afternoon when they rolled through the Crossing and pulled the wagons into the yard behind the livery. Their passage down the street attracted much attention, everybody in town turning out to watch in silence from the wooden sidewalks. Huey Ellis, just coming on duty, ducked through the barn and hurried to where Bentley was unsaddling apart from the others, saying in disbelief,

"I thought you'd pulled out for good . . ."

Bentley flipped him a dollar. "I imagine Herbert did too. Been any sign of him?"

The hostler bobbed his head, bursting to tell his news. "He came in yesterday with his girl and Able Allen and a mean looking crew, and this morning he took the crew out. I heard what he told them, to look for his cattle and if any of the little ranchers had some, to run them out of the country, or if they gave them trouble, to hang them."

"That's nice. Is Able at the bank?"

"'Spect so unless he saw you come in and ducked."

The banker had indeed seen the arrival and at the moment was driving his horse across the river breakneck, to go find Herbert and warn him.

Bentley did not see him leave, busy with dispatching his people, the surveyors to the hotel, the workmen to camp in the vacated shanty town, then he joined the riders waiting by the corral and told them to camp here, near their horses if they should need them in a hurry.

"I want two men to come with me, you, Gordon, and whoever you choose. The rest, go down and wait for me at the courthouse. We won't be long."

Gordon jerked his head at a squat man whose broad face was scarred from many barroom brawls. "Where we going?"

"To the bank to make an arrest."

"Who?"

"The banker, Allen. He blew up the jail to break Herbert out and killed a man."

Gordon laughed, a brittle sound. "Why don't we blow up his bank with him in it? Teach him a lesson and get us some extra dough."

"You're on the other side of the law now Frank, while this job lasts." With men like these he could not afford the familiarity of humor.

Bentley got a grunt for answer and led the pair to the bank, found Allen gone and heard from the frightened clerk that he did not know where his employer was. Bentley made his guess and continued on to the courthouse to pass out badges and swear in his deputies. There was a lot of wry banter as they pinned the badges on, men who had never before seen the back side of a star, and their mood was a restless urgency to explore the new surroundings. Bentley assigned two to guard the wagons and goods and let the rest spread across the town to find amusement.

"Three drinks, no more," he told them. "If anyone gets drunk he's through."

Gordon waited until they had gone, then said sourly, "Don't keep them on too tight a string, friend Bentley. They're a gang of mangy coyotes but you're going to depend on them, maybe a lot."

"Three drinks will get them wet and I don't want to have to depend on a crowd of drunks. I'm going to the hotel and you're on your own for the evening. Change the guard at the livery in a couple of hours to give the boys there a chance at the bar and supper, then relieve them every four hours."

Gordon walked with him and at the hotel used the outside entrance to the saloon. Bentley turned in through the lobby and stopped abruptly. Beth Herbert sat there, an embroidery hoop in her lap, looking up from it at the movement in the doorway. The only other person in the hall was Billy Boils behind the desk. The girl stood up to her full height and walked at Bentley, anger in every fiber of her body, saying in a vicious undertone,

"What are you doing back here, Cal Bentley? Haven't you done enough damage without bringing those cutthroats in here?"

Without answering Cal veered toward the bar, but she veered with him and caught his arm with cruel fingers.

"Don't you dare walk away from me while I'm speaking."

He stopped again, shocked at how ugly her anger made her face, thinking how narrowly he had escaped marrying her, keeping his voice low and even.

"Beth, I am not the one who made this trouble and you know it, and your father is not as smart as I always gave him credit for being. The dam is going to be built and stopping it will not be so simple as killing me the way Ruggles was murdered. Tell this to Boss, the water district is incorporated and the Brown Brothers of Denver are large stockholders. They have more political strength in this state than your father and they will not tolerate his harrassment. Now if you'll excuse me I need a drink to wash out the bad taste in my mouth."

"You," she gasped. "You . . ."

With a wrench he pried her fingers loose and walked through to the saloon leaving her staring, open mouthed, still gasping for words that would not come.

Dude Harris was at the back table with Albert Floyd, morosely watching the new deputies lined along the bar, noisy in their taunts calculated to cow the men of the Crossing. For their part, the townspeople were

171

giving the newcomers a wide berth, which pleased Bentley. He would have his hands full enough controlling the crew in doing the job they were hired for without having to protect the town from them.

He got his drink at the bar and took it to join Dude, sitting where he could see the room, and had lifted the glass to his lips, was swallowing the hot liquid when Beth Herbert walked in and came determinedly toward him. Bentley choked. A hush fell on the room. The local men froze in astonishment that Boss Herbert's daughter would invade their sanctuary but the new riders, seeing her in the mirror, turned about, grinning, and a whistle ran along the bar.

Bentley shoved to his feet, reached her in three strides, got a hand around her upper arm and propelled her back to the lobby unheeding that she stumbled and would have fallen if he had not had hold of her. He walked her out of sight around the desk, swung her to face him and said through stiff white lips.

"I've had enough out of you. You get upstairs and do not come near me again."

Instead she pivoted, swinging within the circle of his arm and wrapped her other arm around his waist, taking a vice grip on his belt, hissing,

"Listen to me, damn you. I wanted to warn you. There's a price on your head. My father is offering a thousand dollars and I don't want your blood on his hands . . . Please . . . Please go away."

Tears filled her eyes and spilled over. Bentley was too furious to care why, whether frustration or worry brought them.

"Thanks. But no."

He broke away, left her there and went back to the table in the saloon. Bending over Dude he said in a low tone,

"Boss is offering a thousand for my head . . . I'm going to ride out to the ranch and see if anything is left."

"You know there ain't." Dude got up. "But what the hell, I'll go along, and Cal, we'd better take some of our friends."

"I mean to."

He pulled four men from the bar, said they were riding and headed the little column to the livery.

There was still a trace of daylight when they put the horses up the mouth of the canyon. Just inside it the downdraft carried the odor of smoke and Dude sniffed it in.

"You got your answer. I'll bet there ain't a stick standing."

"No takers."

But to the amazement of both of them, when they rode through the natural gate the house was standing just as they had left it. Light shone from the windows and smoke curled from the chimney. Bentley stopped the men behind with a raised hand and sat studying the scene, then he discovered that his big corral was filled with cattle. Those would be Box H beeves hazed out of the draws and held here, and whoever was inside would be left here to feed and water them.

He waved his four guards up, explained, and told them, "We'll ride in quietly, each of you take a corner

173

of the house and Dude and I'll go in the back. See that nobody comes out."

They walked the horses across the yard, dropping off two men at the front, the other two circling wide to stay out of the light, Bentley and Dude going with one. As they passed the side window of the kitchen Bentley dismounted and moved in to look through. One man was cooking at One Lung's stove, talking across his shoulder to another at the table. Crouching under the lighted square Bentley waved Dude on around to the rear, then ducked under the window and walked down the side of the house. By the time he turned the corner Dude was already on his feet just outside the kitchen door, his short gun in his hand. He turned his head to watch Bentley come up and when Cal was ready gently eased up the latch and kicked the door inward, stepping through.

The man at the stove swiveled, a hot frying pan in his hand preventing him from reaching for his gun until too late. The seated man half rose and Dude snapped at both of them.

"Stay put."

The half-standing one settled back in the chair, the other eased the smoking pan onto the stove, both of them watchful. It was in their eyes that between them they could take one man, but then Dude stepped aside and Bentley came in.

Leaving Dude to cover them he went first to the man at the stove, told him to face the wall and put his hands on it. He took the gun from the single holster and checked the boot tops, pockets and the nape of his neck

174

for a holdout knife. Not finding one he turned to the table, got the gun and a small knife from the man there. Then he walked quietly through the house looking for anyone else. There was no one. At the front door he whistled the deputies in, then went back to question the pair in the kitchen.

He asked first where Boss Herbert was and got the sullen answer that neither knew, they had been alone here four days with no word from anyone, rounding up cattle. They were not members of the old Box H crew.

He stepped back as the deputies appeared, ordered the pair trussed in chairs, then sent his men to open the corral and scatter the animals for an hour. While they were gone Bentley and Dude put together a supper for them all, to eat before they took the prisoners down to the Crossing.

CHAPTER
SIXTEEN

Boss Herbert with the bulk of his augmented crew had made their camp in the old ranch yard. Every time he looked at or smelled the charred ruin of his buildings he hated Cal Bentley more, and that was why he chose to stay here. The emotion was like food to him, nourishing his determination that Snakeshead Valley should be his exclusively again.

The chuck wagon was drawn up close to where the blacksmith shop had stood and they were cooking on the forge. In the waning daylight Herbert filled his plate with beef and beans, speared a chuck of camp bread and found a seat on the wagon tongue. The range meat was tough but his big teeth chewed on it with relish, as though he were chewing on Cal Bentley himself. That was the only food he was hungry for.

The sound of a horse running on the hard ground grew, coming in, then the animal kicked up dust as it appeared from behind the wagon and was hauled up, dancing. Able Allen threw himself out of the saddle, dropped the reins and stood panting in front of Herbert, saying between breaths,

"Bentley's back."

Herbert swallowed his mouthful and a slow, heavy smile stretched his big lips. "So much the better, I don't have to hunt him."

The banker wagged his head, trying to get enough air to talk, and managed, "He isn't alone. He brought a crew that looks just as rough as this one."

Herbert filled his mouth again and said around the food, "How many?"

"I didn't take time to count. A lot. And he brought a whole caravan along, teamsters, laborers, scrapers. It looks like he means to build that dam himself."

"Not while I'm alive he won't. Sit down before you fall down." Herbert speared his fork at the tongue. "Where do you suppose he got the people?"

Allen sat down, straightening his clothes, breathing deeply and more slowly and talking more easily. "I recognized one rider. He was pointed out to me in the Holladay Street fall they call the Slaughter House. Frank Gordon."

"What is he?"

"Killer. Gambler. Con man. Denver is full of men like him."

"Who all like money. We can handle him. Whatever Bentley is paying him I'll double it, buy them off and get rid of them."

Allen did not enjoy hearing money talked of so casually and he cautioned, "But Bentley could just hire more."

"Go bring me some coffee while I think," Herbert told the banker, and when Allen brought the cup said, "better have him stay around until we run Bentley down so he doesn't get suspicious. Get yourself some grub then ride in and bring Gordon here. I'll talk to him."

Allen fidgeted, not wanting to go back to the Crossing with Cal Bentley there and he coughed a protest. "I think you ought to send somebody else, if Bentley sees me he's apt to shoot me for blowing the jail."

Boss Herbert understood. He did not approve his daughter's taste in men, but until he had this battle won and was again master of the valley he needed the banker and the loans he could browbeat out of him. When it was over he could talk some sense into the girl or send her away to break up the affair. At the moment though it gave him a wry pleasure to make the man squirm.

"You'll manage. Get word to Beth to contact this Gordon, have him meet you. I don't care how you do it but bring him out here."

Allen got a plate for himself and ate without appetite, trying to think of an argument that would relieve him of this errand, but when he had finished he could only say lamely,

"I damn near killed my horse coming out. He can't make it back . . ."

Herbert raised a bellow that a fresh horse be caught up and Allen's saddle thrown on it, then added another barb. "Try to get back in three or four hours. I want this buttoned up tonight."

Grinning, he watched Allen mount and ride off, pleased as he had not been by anything since the first suit had been filed against him.

178

Able Allen was considerably less than pleased. He had a special fear of Cal Bentley. He had taken the lawyer's girl and ever since he had expected Bentley to make some move against him. Now he had more to fear since Josh Roebuck had been killed. If he ran into Bentley the least he could expect would be arrest. The worst would be a bullet or a rope around his neck. Short on courage, Allen relied on his brain, but during the whole ride to the Crossing it did not help him solve this situation.

At least it was full dark when he rode in. He kept to the back way, along the river bank behind the buildings that faced the main street, reached his house safely and stabled his horse, then ducked through the shadows to where his clerk lived and knocked at the rear door. Ten minutes worth of pounding brought no answer. He had to have a messenger. He could not risk walking into the hotel for Beth where the odds were good that he would run into Bentley.

Then he thought of Huey Ellis who had run errands for him before. But he could not use either the street or the alley because Bentley's wagons were in the livery yard and probably guarded. He hurried back along the river bank, stopped at the main corner to look along the street and finding it empty darted across to the runway and into the office, he thought without being seen. He found Huey reading a tattered magazine and rang a dollar on the desk.

"Go to the hotel, Huey, find my Beth and tell her to meet me at my place as soon as she can, but don't let anyone else know."

He did not linger there where Bentley might show up, but slipped back the way he had come and sat down in his porch chair, swallowed by the blackness under the roof.

Huey Ellis marked the page in his magazine, dropped it on the desk and went out after Allen toward the hotel, gnawed at by curiosity. What was Allen doing back in town and what was so all fired important that the tight-fisted galoot would give him a dollar to send for his girl in such secrecy? A true gossip, Huey kept a close track of whatever happened at the Crossing and his nose itched to find out what was going on.

The girl was in the lobby with her embroidery but the delicate work could not calm her nerves. She did not know where her father was, or Able Allen or Cal Bentley, and the explosiveness of the situation had her on a fine edge of fright. Huey Ellis came up on the porch, put his head through the open door and hissed at her and she jumped, her hands flying wide. Then she saw him, saw him beckon and said,

"What do you want? Come here and say it." The voice had a sharp asperity as a reaction to being so startled.

Huey shook his head, put a finger against his lips and beckoned again impatiently. Fear of what his message might be brought her to her feet and she went quickly to the door and out. On the porch Huey lifted to his toes to speak close to her ear in a clandestine tone.

"Able Allen wants you to come to his place right away and not let anybody know."

He turned away and almost ran toward the barn, but when he reached the cross street he looked back. The girl was not in sight and Huey sprinted into the side street then circled around to Allen's house through the alley and sidled along the wall to the front corner. The girl was just climbing the front steps. Huey heard her anxious, low call.

"Able?"

Allen stood up in the deep shadow, saying, "Here, Beth," and went forward to take her in his arms.

Through the pickets of the porch railing Huey Ellis thought his kiss was too perfunctory, that this was more than a love tryst, and strained to listen. Allen said without preamble,

"There's a man in town your father wants to talk to, Frank Gordon. He rode in with Bentley today. I want you to find him and bring him here."

The girl backed out of the banker's arms stiffly. "Why, Able?"

"To make a deal with him."

She caught her breath and her voice was harsh. "To buy him off? So Cal Bentley can be killed? Oh . . . no thank you, I am not having any of that."

Allen caught her arm in his impatience. "Beth, whose side are you on? You can't walk both sides of the street and it's either Bentley or your father. Do you want Boss killed?"

"Of course not. I don't want either . . ."

"Go to the hotel and send Gordon here to me if you don't want a blood bath in the Crossing." He turned her about and all but shoved her down the steps.

She stood on the path twisting her hands together for a long moment until Allen said, "Go," as though he were ordering a dog to fetch. Then to Huey's astonishment she went docilely down the path. Allen sat down again and Huey huddled below the porch hardly daring to breathe until ten minutes later a chilling voice spoke from the darkness at the other end of the porch.

"Allen?"

"Gordon? I want to offer you a better deal than you're getting." Allen spoke hurriedly in case Bentley had named him as a target to his crew, to stave off being shot out of hand.

The other man too was wary. "Get out where I can see you and keep your hands away from your sides."

Allen got up and walked reluctantly to the steps where the faint starlight made him a gray figure, the hands lifted to shoulder level. A tall man appeared, facing him. One second there had been no one on the path and now there was.

"Talk." The voice was cold.

Allen's words had a quake as he said, "Boss Herbert wants you to ride out to his camp with me so he can . . ."

A harsh laugh interrupted him. "Kill me?"

"I could have had you shot right here if that was what Boss wanted. But why should he?"

"You know I work for Bentley."

"That can be changed. If you switch sides Herbert will pay you twice what you're getting now."

There was a hesitation, then a chuckle. "You want me to murder the man I'm riding for?"

"No, just keep your crowd from butting in when Herbert comes for him tonight."

"Very funny, Mac. I figure we got quite a long job ahead of us at fancy wages. You knock Bentley off tonight and what do we get paid for? Half a day? What kind of an idiot do you take me to be?"

Huey Ellis could nearly feel Allen sweating and his voice was tight with the pressure.

"If you'll just talk to Herbert he'll make it very worth your while. Get your horse and ride across the ford, meet me beyond the shanty town over there. It's important that we aren't seen together, Bentley must not be warned."

Huey Ellis had heard enough. If Gordon did not come to the livery it would mean he had refused Allen, but if he did come Huey wanted to be in the barn office when he got there. He backed carefully along the wall, then ran down the alley, into the office, dropped in his chair and grabbed up his magazine.

He had pretended to read one page and turned it when boots scuffed in the runway and Frank Gordon took the lighted lantern off the nail and carried it to the stall to saddle his horse. Huey did not move. He saw the glow increase as the mounted man returned the lantern, heard the hoofs muffled in the dust walk out of the runway. It was Huey's turn to sweat. Cal Bentley had ridden out of town and not come back and Ellis knew no way to warn him nor who would find him first.

★ ★ ★

Frank Gordon crossed the ford and walked his animal through the dark shack town where Bentley's laborers were sleeping. A quarter mile beyond the last building Able Allen waited beside the trail. Without speaking he turned his horse east and they rode at an easy trot until the embers of the fire located Herbert's camp.

"Wait here," Allen told the special deputy. "I'll bring Boss out. The fewer people know about the meeting the less chance of a leak to Bentley."

Frank Gordon eased himself in the saddle and built a smoke while Allen rode on. The Box H crew were dark shapes rolled in their blankets but Boss Herbert paced the yard close to the corral where his saddled horse was tied. He heard Allen coming, mounted and rode out to intercept him, saw he was alone and cursed.

"You didn't bring him?"

"He's waiting back a ways. I thought you'd want to see him alone."

"Yeah. He bought the deal then?"

"You'll have to sweeten it to get him. He expected to work a long time, not just through the night."

"No problem," Herbert grunted and rode on toward the glow of the cigarette hanging at the corner of Frank Gordon's mouth.

He could see no more of the man than that he was tall and lean but he cared nothing what he looked like. The voice would tell him enough.

"I'm Herbert," he said. "What's Bentley paying you?"

A disinterested drawl came back. "Two hundred a month to me, a hundred and found to the rest. Every month."

184

"I'll double that. And you can all ride for me while I put my ranch back together."

"That sounds better. But how do I know you'll pay anything after you get Bentley?"

"I'll give you an order on Allen's bank tonight for the first month in advance."

"Write it out then and I'll go pull out my crew before Bentley gets back."

"He's not in town?" Herbert's voice sharpened. "Where is he?"

"Rode out with his foreman and four of my men this afternoon, I don't know where to."

Herbert asked Allen for paper and a pencil, struck a match and wrote the order on his thigh and passed it to Gordon.

"I don't want your crew pulled out. I want them around so he thinks you're still his. When he gets back watch your chance to grab him and send me word. We'll come pick him up."

"You're on. I'd better ride. I don't want him thinking I've been anywhere this long and wondering why."

Gordon swung away and rode smartly for the Crossing. Herbert listened to the receding sound until it faded, then told Allen,

"Go on back and keep an eye on him, see if he does tell his crowd there's a change or if he doublecrosses me and tells Bentley. And don't cash that order until you're sure."

Herbert returned to his camp and changed the guard he had posted when Allen had told him of Bentley's reappearance in the town, warning the new sentries to be especially alert. If Gordon did go to Bentley they could expect an attack within hours. Then he rolled in his blankets and went to sleep.

Able Allen followed Frank Gordon at a distance. Against the roaring rush of the river he could hear nothing, but the brilliance of the summer stars cast light enough across the meadow that he could make out the moving shape ahead from time to time. Gordon headed straight for town and was crossing the ford as Allen reached the upper end of the shanty town. Allen walked his horse on to the water's edge, waited until Gordon turned into the main street, passing in front of the lighted windows there, then put his own horse across the shallow water and up the bank to the street level. At the corner he was in time to see the rump of Gordon's animal disappear into the livery. Allen crossed the main street to the alley mouth and stopped there where he could look along to the livery yard. If Gordon was going to keep his bargain he would probably talk first to the guards there watching the wagons, then go on to find the others.

Shortly the banker saw the tall figure come into the yard and approach the man leaning against the corral, speak with him briefly, then move on to one on the far side of the yard. That satisfied Allen. He did not want to use the alley and let Gordon see him spying, and with that route cut off and the main street too dangerous, he turned back toward the ford to ride along the bank to his house. Half way down the block a group of riders came up the bank just in front of him.

186

Cal Bentley and his foreman with six men behind them whom Allen did not know.

He tried to turn his horse to run. It was only halfway around when Dude Harris's rope fell over him and was snagged tight, but the horse kept turning. Able was yanked from the saddle and fell, the wind knocked out of him when he landed on the gritty street.

Dude dallied the rope around his horn, told the horse to stand and dropped down, his short gun in his hand when he touched the ground. He bent over the banker, found and lifted his gun and stood back, saying with satisfaction.

"You can get up now."

Able Allen got to his feet slowly, shaken by the fall and hearing Dude call to Bentley.

"Do we hang him now or make it a show in the morning?"

CHAPTER
SEVENTEEN

"Quit clowning, Dude," Bentley said, and then to Allen, "get on your horse, Able, I'm going to lock you up."

With Frank Gordon's crew near and since he was not going to be killed at once, Able found the courage to sneer at the captors.

"You won't hold me for long."

"We'll see." Bentley backed his horse to the men behind him and said, "We'll take them over to the courthouse now."

The four deputies of course had not heard from Gordon, but Allen mounted confidently and rode to the jail, Harris close behind him holding his gun loosely across his saddle. As he got down his eyes slid along the face of the building, saw that the wall had been repaired, and walked inside ahead of Dude. Bentley lighted a lamp and Allen had his first good look at the other two prisoners. He did not know either, so they must be some of the new men Boss Herbert had put on. The deputies untied their wrists and shoved them toward the cell, but one hung back to protest to Bentley.

188

"Mister, I don't know what this is all about. What are you charging us with? We didn't do anything but round up some cows like Mr. Herbert told us. That ain't no crime."

"Trespassing is," Bentley said shortly.

"Trespassing where?"

"In my house. Cooking my grub. Go on, get into that cell."

Sullenly they filed in and Bentley jerked his head at Allen and after a look at the storm in Bentley's face the banker thought it prudent not to press his luck just now and followed the riders. Dude locked the grille and dropped the key in the top drawer of the new desk.

Bentley told his deputies, "All of you stay here. Two can sleep while the others watch." He indicated the couch and chairs, "but I want two men awake at all times. Able Allen there threw dynamite through this window to break Boss Herbert out and killed a deputy of mine. I don't want a repeat in case Herbert has come in."

It made an impression. Bentley and Dude left the building and Dude ran a rope through the bridles of the seven horses, mounted his own and with Bentley beside him led the string to the livery.

Huey Ellis startled them, jumping out of a chair in the darkness outside the runway door, catching Bentley's bridle and whispering hoarsely,

"Don't go in there. Don't get down. That Gordon bastard sold you out. The guards back in the yard are laying for you."

Cold washed through Cal Bentley and he leaned toward the low sound of Ellis's voice to ask,

"Are you sure? How do you know?"

"I'm sure all right. Able Allen came sneaking in here after dark and gave me a dollar to tell Beth Herbert to meet him at his house in a hurry. That ain't like Allen and I got curious, lucky for you. I went up and listened to them. Allen told her to send Gordon to him and she did. I waited until he came and Allen offered him twice what you're paying his crew to change sides and not let you know. Gordon wanted more and Allen told him to ride out to Herbert's camp with him to make a deal. I ducked back here and sure enough, Gordon comes for his horse and takes off. When he comes back he goes out and talks to the men in the yard, then he heads up the street. He's at the hotel now. You'd better clear out of town quick."

"That's for sure, Cal," Dude said. "As soon as I kill that *special deputy.*"

Futility made Bentley sound exhausted. Whatever he did, Boss Herbert was able to counter and ruin. He told Harris,

"A waste of time that we haven't got. Go back to the shanty town and tell those men the job is sour for now. Tell them to clear out, there's no use in any of them getting hurt. Then meet me at the hotel. The back."

"The hotel?" Dude's breath sucked in. "You damn fool, the whole doublecrossing crew is there at the bar I bet."

"I know. But they won't make their play that public. They'll want to catch me alone where nobody can stop them."

"But why? What do you want to go there for?"

"Clothes. Food. And to send the surveyors away."

Dude Harris cursed bitterly. "So Able Allen knew better than he let on why he wouldn't stay in jail for long. We should have strung him up while we had the chance."

Cal Bentley almost agreed. Between the banker and rancher they had whipsawed him ever since he had come home with the court order he had been so sure would pull Boss Herbert's fangs. Now . . . Now, what was there left to do? The immediate need was to get out of the Crossing, hide out somewhere where he could think, look for yet another solution. Because he was going to build that dam. He dug through his pockets and held a handful of coins toward Huey Ellis.

"Fan these extra horses off somewhere, Huey, so you won't be involved. And thanks."

"I don't want that money, Cal. You know why I feel like I do about Herbert . . . You better move before one of those guards gets nosey."

Dude Harris was already crossing the ford and Ellis took the lead rope from Bentley, pulled it out of the reins and fanned the animals off into the dark down the street. Bentley put his horse toward the riverbank and around to the back of the hotel, remembering Huey Ellis's little spread up at the head of Snakeshead Valley. Boss Herbert had hurrahed him off, appropriated his small herd and made his barn and house a storage place for winter feed and shelter for his own crew while they worked the upper area. There were many such men hanging on in the back canyons, hating Herbert. Perhaps he could get help there.

He walked deliberately to the front of the hotel and into the lobby, hoping that his guess was right that his late deputies would not move against him under the watching eyes of whatever townspeople were still in the saloon. Frank Gordon was the first person he saw, seated in a lobby chair, his long legs stretched out and his hat down over his face as if he were asleep. He was not sleeping. At the sound of Bentley's steps he straightened and shoved the hat back.

"Where you been all this while?"

The man's eyes evaded him and there was a tension in the way he brought his legs under him, ready to spring up. Cal thought it might be because his having been out of town all evening suggested that he might have been watching Herbert's camp and been a witness to Gordon's meeting with Herbert. He kept his voice casual.

"Riding. How come you're all by yourself here?"

"I been waiting for your orders."

"I'll have some in the morning. Go on to bed."

Gordon shoved up slowly, plainly trying to make up his mind whether he could take Bentley now but taking too long about it. His moment passed and he turned toward the stairs. Bentley watched him go, not relaxing, his hand hanging near his gun until the man disappeared in the upper hall and he heard a door open and close. Then he went softly up the steps, to the room where he had left the new clothes he had brought from Denver. He was very glad for the sheep-lined coats. It would be chill in the high hills where he intended going.

He unlocked the door, went in and closed it quietly, then quickly shoved the clothes into the duffel bag, stripped the blankets off the beds and stowed them in. He closed and tied the mouth of the bag and started out.

Frank Gordon was standing in the open doorway, his gun leveled on Bentley's middle. Bentley had not heard the latch lifted. The man was an artful burglar, his grin wolfish.

"Going someplace again?"

Bentley stood still, saying nothing.

"Turn around. Let go that bag."

Bentley dropped the cord and turned. There was nothing else to do. The voice spoke to his back.

"Ease out your gun and drop it." When Bentley had done that Gordon chuckled. "Now walk toward the wall, stop three feet from it and lean your weight on your right arm."

Bentley obeyed, not knowing what the man intended. A minute later a buckskin thong was looped around his left wrist, the arm pulled up behind him and the thong twisted around his neck. He was as effectively tied as if he were wrapped in miles of rope. If he took his hand off the wall he would fall on his face. If he tried to straighten, the arm behind him would tighten and choke him.

Gordon's low laugh mocked him. "On Holladay Street we call that the poor man's handcuff."

He was not finished, now fastening a second thong around Bentley's right wrist and yanking the hand away from the wall. Cal fell, his head slamming against the wall and sliding down it until he landed on his knees. Gordon whipped the loose end of the new thong around an ankle and pulled it tight, forcing Cal to roll on his side, twisted and cramped. Gordon stood up, surveyed him critically and said in satisfaction,

"I guess that will hold you while I send word for Herbert to come pick you up."

"I don't believe I would, Frank."

Cal Bentley heard the voice and almost laughed in relief. He squirmed to look up and saw Dude Harris just inside the door. Gordon had been so confident that he started and was late in whipping around. By the time he moved Dude had put two bullets in his back. The man staggered a step toward him before he collapsed and Dude put two more bullets in the head, just in case. Then he looked at Bentley.

"Well if you ain't a trussed up turkey." Keeping his gun in one hand he drew his knife with the other and sliced through the thongs. "Cute little boy, wasn't he?"

Doors were slamming up and down the hall. Bentley rolled up to his feet, jumped for his gun and the duffel bag, said, "Let's get out of here," and ran to the hall.

He almost butted down Beth Herbert. She gaped at him, at the gun, gasped, "Cal . . . What . . . ?" then saw the crumpled body beyond him and understood.

194

Cal dodged around her, saying, "Tell Boss the game isn't played out yet," and brushed by with Dude on his heels.

Boots were pounding across the lobby from the saloon. Bentley ran for the rear stairs and down them to the kitchen, left Dude to hold the narrow doorway and went on to the big press where the hotel larder was stored. He found a burlap sack and threw into it beans, flour, coffee, a few cans of peaches. He heard the boots overhead, then they came clattering down the steps and he swung back to the roomy kitchen in time to see Dude Harris throw down on the first of the deputies.

Bentley covered the door to the dining room but there was no sound from there. Dude drew the men out of the stairwell, their hands raised. There were three of them, late stayers from the saloon who had had many more than three drinks but were not too drunk to respect Dude's gun.

"In here." Bentley motioned to the pantry.

Dude marched them over and Bentley took their guns, then shoved them inside, sullen, glowering men. The last one held back to ask,

"What the hell was the shooting?"

"Gordon. He's dead and you will be too if you don't get in there and stay quiet." He pushed the man in the back with his gun barrel, shut the door and blocked it with a chair back tipped under the knob, and said loudly enough to be heard through it, "See they stay put, Dude, I'll be down in a minute."

He ran up the stairs and pushed through the people crowded in the hall until he located a member of the

195

survey team, told him quickly that the guards had sold them out and warned them to clear out of town with the laborers.

"Take everything back to Denver and turn it over to the Brown brothers. I don't think Herbert will bother you on the road but he'll probably stop you long enough to learn that I'm not with you. Let him look. Don't try to argue with him."

"I'd rather argue with the devil," the surveyor said. "Some job this was."

Bentley returned to the kitchen. There was no sound from the pantry and he beckoned to Dude. With the sack of food and the duffel they tiptoed to the rear door and out to the horses.

They raced their animals to the ford and across it and drove through the shanty town where lamps burned and the men were hurriedly making ready to leave. Beyond the shacks Bentley headed north.

"Where we going?" Dude asked.

"Up Mount Tom. There are plenty of places to hide and it's high enough that we can see anyone who comes up looking for us."

They were beginning to climb when dawn drew its first pink line above the crest. At seven o'clock they stopped beside a trickle of water falling toward the Whitewater, let the horses drink and ate a cold breakfast, afraid that smoke from the smallest fire could betray them. By noon even with the overhead sun the altitude chilled the air and a downdraft made it colder. They dug out the sheep-lined coats and Dude tied his bandana over his hat, pulling the brim close over his ears. Bentley wanted to do the same but it was important that he be able to hear any first faint suspicious sound.

They mounted again and rode higher, until the timber thinned and the valley lay in a sweeping spread below them, the craggy range of mountains on the opposite side of Tom rolled to the horizon. And there they set up camp.

CHAPTER
EIGHTEEN

Able Allen rode into Boss Herbert's camp at ten in the morning in a seething rage. He had spent the night in the jail until the deputies broke out of the pantry, routed all those still sleeping, counted noses and found four missing. It had taken a while longer to discover where they were, to tell them of the new deal with Herbert and that Frank Gordon was dead, to release the men in the cell. Allen told them to stay in town and wait for orders from Herbert.

Herbert listened to the account of the night with his mouth clamped shut. When he heard that the teamsters, the laborers and surveyors had vanished he called his crew to the saddle and rode hard for the Crossing. The information he wanted most and that no one had was whether Bentley had gone with the caravan. Even the two who had guarded the wagons had been overwhelmed by the number of men appearing out of the night and had drifted away, had not seen Bentley if he was among them.

The Box H whirled up before the hotel and before Herbert dismounted his daughter hurried out to the porch, the anxiety in her face giving way to relief when she saw both Boss and Able Allen. Herbert swung down and caught her hands.

"You all right, honey? Somebody told Able you saw that Gordon shot."

Leaning against him the girl said tightly, "No, I got there just afterward. Cal and Dude Harris were running out of the room . . . I don't know which one did it."

"Do you know where Bentley's construction gang went?"

"I don't, but Huey Ellis must have seen them leave."

Herbert bawled to the nearest rider to bring Ellis and gave his attention back to Beth to be sure she was not still shaken by the killing, comforting her until a reluctant Huey Ellis arrived, then left her to Allen, saying brusquely to Ellis,

"You see those teamsters pull out?"

Huey wanted to be cautious, not to say too much, to trip himself up. "I heard them."

"Didn't see them?"

"Well . . . sort of . . ."

"What do you mean by that?"

"It was still dark and I was half asleep. They waked me up yelling and harnessing and I went to the back door, but I was in my sock feet and I didn't think it was any of my business anyhow."

Herbert knew this man, knew that Huey would poke his nose into anything that caught his curiosity and he switched his questioning.

"You do know Dude and Bentley killed Frank Gordon?"

"I heard so later. Is it true? I thought he was part of their crowd."

Herbert ignored that and probed on. "Did you see them around those wagons?"

"Sure didn't. Maybe they rode out of town and waited for them to come along."

"Did you hear where the mob was headed?"

"Nothing about that, but they came from Denver so I'd guess they're going back."

Not satisfied but not wanting to waste more time on the barn man, Herbert flapped a hand at Beth and Allen, mounted and took his crew out of the Crossing at a run. Although the wagons had a five hour start he caught them where they had halted for a noon meal and stopped his crew fifty yards short, got down with Joe Garvey and walked at the men who gathered into a group as if for protection. They were a nervous bunch. A few wore guns but no one showed any interest in a tangle with the Box H.

As soon as he could be heard Herbert called ahead, "Who's the boss man here?"

A tall, broad shouldered, black haired man said, "There ain't none but I'll do to speak for us. What do you want?"

The words were bold, blunt, and Herbert was not used to being spoken to in that tone but he shrugged off the annoyance, in single-minded determination.

"We're looking for Cal Bentley and Dude Harris. They here?"

"Nope."

"We'll look."

"Help yourself." The man turned his back, walked to the fire and poured coffee for himself.

The wagons were strung down the road, the horses unhitched and tethered to the wheels and Herbert and Garvey took them one at a time, pulling back the canvas hoods, hoping but not really believing they would find the pair cowering inside. The search was quickly made, then they returned to the watching construction men and Herbert singled out the man who had spoken before.

"Sure they weren't with you and lit out when they saw us coming?"

"Sure."

"Where did they go then?"

"Only thing I know about them is, Harris came and waked us up, said he and Bentley were taking off because Frank Gordon had sold out to you."

"He knew that? How did he find out?"

"Search me. He just said we'd better move as soon as we could, then he went away and in a few minutes we heard shots."

"That was when they killed Gordon. But how did they know about him?"

"Mister, they didn't tell me and I never was much of a mind reader."

"You see either of them after the shooting?"

"No, and I wasn't looking for them. I was busy loading up."

At any other time Boss Herbert would not have let that kind of lip go unpunished, but just now he was too concerned with where Bentley and Harris were to take notice of trifles.

Walking back to the crew Joe Garvey growled, "Maybe they weren't here and maybe they were. I'm going to have some boys scout around up ahead, see if there's any sign they jumped off in the brush."

He sent two men to ride slowly along each side of the string of wagons and search the ground, but in an hour of looking they found nothing except the tracks of normal travel on the road. Herbert accepted the report and gave up on this possibility and they rode back to the Crossing. As they came into town Joe Garvey had another idea, one that shocked him into cursing.

"Boss, you know something? It would be mighty like Bentley to have raided our camp while we been off looking for him."

Herbert yanked his horse to a stop, his spine straightening in apprehension, his blazing eyes looking ahead at a scene he could envision, then he shook his head thoughtfully and told his foreman,

"Maybe, but I doubt it. I don't think he'd waste the time when he thinks both my crew and his are on his tail. I think they've ridden clear out, that we're shut of them."

Garvey did not let go of the idea, insisting, "At least let's send the boys out to see."

Herbert agreed to that and the crew was dispatched with orders to send a message back if the camp had been molested, to stay there for the night if it had not, then he and Garvey dropped off at the saloon, dry from the long day of riding.

They chose a table at the rear, Herbert sitting where he would not have to look at the sodden figure of Floyd Albert, always an irritation to him when he was in the best of moods, and his mood now was anything but light. He noted three strangers at the bar, gunslinger written on all of them, and was not surprised when one walked to his table with an insolent swagger and said.

"You Boss Herbert?"

Herbert looked up stonily and barely nodded.

"Frank Gordon told us you'd put us on your payroll at two hundred and found. You going to keep the bargain?"

"Not that one. Gordon is dead and the job Bentley hired you for is washed out." He watched the man's eyes turn hot and he was too tired to ask for a fight tonight and went on, "I'll give you a choice. I'll take you on at Bentley's wages or you can pull your string. Either way, but if you stay around here you ride for me. Take your pick."

The man lingered a moment as if he would argue, then shrugged and went back to consult with the other two. Herbert had a second drink while he watched them. He did not need them if Bentley was gone, but unless they were on his payroll he wanted them out of the country where Bentley could not get to them again in case he was still around. The conference did not last long and the man came back to say,

"It's too damn dead around here to suit us. We'll drift."

"Make it tonight. I'll hang any of you who are here in the morning."

Herbert got up, turned his broad back on the man and walked toward the lobby door. The man flushed as though Herbert had slapped him and his hand dropped toward his gun. Joe Garvey's voice hit at him.

"Don't try."

The gunslinger turned his head, saw Garvey's gun in his hand above the table and let his clawed fingers relax and drop. "Hell with you," he said, and went out through the street door.

Garvey's attention swept to the bar and the two there. They had been caught with glasses in their hands with no time to put them down and draw and they faced Garvey's gun rigidly. Garvey's rage to kill seized him as it had for years, but it was only sparked to action when he was challenged and he waited, hoping one of the men would give him the slightest opportunity. They did not. Even across the room they recognized the signals and with utmost care they stepped away from the bar and carried the glasses with them out of the saloon.

Garvey fought the urge down, holstered his gun and followed Herbert. The lobby was empty except for the smell of fresh baked bread from the dining room, and suddenly Garvey was ravenous. The surge of that rage always had that effect on him.

Herbert, his daughter, and Able Allen were already at a table where a fourth chair was empty. Garvey took it unasked and saw the flash of annoyance cross Beth's face. She had never liked the foreman's arrogance nor her father's treating him as a member of the family. He had lived in the big house rather than with the rest of the crew, had eaten at the family table and he had never been particular in washing and shaving. Garvey ignored her. He knew exactly how she felt and it was a matter of indifference to him. He considered her a spoiled brat and in her childhood he with everyone else had had to bear her temper tantrums. He said to Able,

"No word in town about Bentley and Harris?"

"Nothing. My guess is they're on their way to Denver. What can they do without men and equipment?"

"It was Dude who told them to pull out. I wonder why?"

They were silent while the waitress served them, then Herbert said, "Because we showed Bentley he can't beat me any way he tries. He's given up. I expect he'll go to Denver and practice law up there."

Joe Garvey spoke with his mouth full of beans. "I don't believe it. That jasper never did know how to quit."

"Then where is he?"

The foreman pointed over his shoulder with his fork. "Could be he went back to his hardscrabble spread in the canyon."

"Why? He's got to know I won't let him stay there any longer. What would he think he could do?"

"I don't know." Garvey shook his head, chasing his mouth with a thick slice of buttered bread. "I've just got a feeling about him."

Able Allen scoffed. "You and your feelings . . . Boss is right, in a week or so we'll hear he's in the capital." He pushed his chair back, rose and helped Beth to her feet. "We're going to the Crowells's to play cards so I can forget I ever knew Cal Bentley." He started to turn away, then turned back, taking a paper from his pocket. "Oh, Boss, I went to Moss's and got this money order back from Gordon."

Joe Garvey's face was sour as he watched them leave and he growled, "Maybe you're going to quit looking for Bentley but I'm going up that canyon tonight."

Boss Herbert studied his foreman and said in a flat voice, "I didn't say I was quitting. I'll ride with you, tonight, tomorrow and every day until I learn where he is. If he's in this country we'll dig him out."

They finished their supper, stopped at the bar for a handful of cigars, and went out to the hitch rail, Garvey breaking one cigar in half, settling one piece in his cheek and dropping the other in his pocket. Their first stop was at the livery, where Huey Ellis assured them that Bentley's deputies had come for their horses and ridden out. Then they crossed the ford. As they passed through the deserted community on the far side Herbert told Garvey,

"Burn this trash heap out this week."

It was full dark when they rode up Bentley's canyon and reined in at the narrow mouth, moving through it cautiously. There was no light in the log house, no odor of smoke, and when they rode around it there were no animals in the corral. The rising new moon showed it to be empty. The last time Boss Herbert had been here the big enclosure had been filled with his cattle and a new flush of anger started him cursing Cal Bentley again.

206

Garvey had gone on into the house, struck a match and lit a kitchen lamp. When Herbert joined him he had made a search of the pantry and expressed the opinion that the men they sought had been here recently and stripped the larder of a good deal of food.

"Maybe," Herbert was less sure. "Or it could have been our boys using it while they gathered the stock. We'll spend the night here and look around some more in the morning."

"I'll make you a bet," the foreman said doggedly, "that when it's light we'll find sign they were here today."

But when day came the only tracks they found were their own coming in, overlaying a muddle of prints heading down trail, which would have been left when Bentley's posse had taken the two Box H riders down to jail them.

"Never mind," Boss Herbert told a savagely angry Garvey, "we'll go pick up the crew and comb everything until he turns up somewhere."

CHAPTER
NINETEEN

For two weeks Cal Bentley and Dude Harris moved by night through the rough land to the east of the big valley, seeking out the hill ranchers, riding to one place after another and making careful surveys before they approached to be sure they would not run into any Box H men.

The people they talked to all had reason to hate Boss Herbert. Bentley argued the importance of the dam, pointing out that when it was complete they could take up land against the newly created reservoir and make a decent living again instead of barely scraping by. All of them wanted the dam but not one would stand against Boss Herbert to make it possible. The unanimous opinion was that they were not making much where they were but at least they were alive. At the beginning of the third week one man repeated the line and added,

"I'll tell you something else, Bentley, unless you quit ramming around like this you ain't gonna be. Box H was by here some days ago. Boss got wind you're still in the area and raised his ante. There's five thousand for the man who turns you over to Herbert or brings him your body. He don't make no bones that he'd rather have you dead. And Roper's listening. He came over wanting me to help him catch you."

Bentley was very conscious of the man's patched clothes, his broken hat and cracked boots. Gardner had three small children, ran only a handful of cows, and the meager hillside soil supported a bad joke of a garden.

"Why didn't you throw in with him?"

The man's faded eyes pleaded. "I don't want no blood money. But Mr. Bentley, I just can't join you. I ain't got much to live for but I ain't ready to commit suicide and I'd sure do that if Boss heard I was helping you."

"I understand . . . And your warning is a help. Thanks."

This was the last of the little ranchers. There was nowhere in the territory left to turn for support. As they rode out of Gardner's yard Dude Harris sounded hopeless.

"Well, this is the end of it. Damn but I want one crack at Herbert."

"You'll get it." Bentley's voice was harder than Dude had ever heard it. "We'll go back to Denver and get an army of federal marshals if I have to hold a gun on the governor and the United States Marshal for the southern district of Colorado both."

"I'm for getting out of here anyway. If these hill people are watching for us somebody's going to spot us and go after that five thousand."

"That is exactly why we can't get out now. What we'll have to do is go back up the mountain and lie low there long enough to convince everybody we're gone and they quit watching the trails so closely. From the camp we can at least see who all is hunting us."

Through the next few days it was evident that the hunt was on in deadly earnest. Scouting parties scoured the main valley and climbed the side canyons in a methodical network. Sooner or later someone was bound to climb the mountain. There were several ways down but it was certain that all of them were being watched.

Cal Bentley paced the campsite, restless as a caged cat. He climbed a steep pile of loose boulders to look down at the mountain's foot as he had done daily. This time, a rock he trusted his weight to rolled and dropped him ten feet to the stones on the floor of the bowl and fell on top of him. His hip was bruised so badly that he could not sit a saddle, could not even walk.

For a week he lay in agony. Dude kept watch and daily reported that the net was closing, that the searchers had almost reached the base of the mountain. Further, they were running low on food. They had no coffee, only a part of the sack of beans, a little jerked meat, all together not enough to last more than a very few days."

"The closest place to get grub is the ranch," Dude said. "I can make it down tonight . . ."

Bentley sat up hurriedly and dropped back as pain shot through him. "That's the last place to go, Dude. Herbert will have that staked out for sure. Maybe you could get to Luck's Bluff though. There's no sign that they've been over that way. We're short on cash, but take this ring."

At one time Luck's Bluff had been a thriving mining camp a day's ride north of the head of Snakeshead Valley. It clung on top of a bluff above the Whitewater where the river cut through a gorge so narrow that it crowded the river into a channel forty feet deep that sluiced toward the easier grade into the valley. The roar of it was a constant thunder in the air.

From their camp the old community could only be reached by winding cattle and deer trails that dropped into the cross canyons, climbed and dropped to the next. It was not an easy trip, but the very roughness of it made it less likely that Dude would be discovered, for the bulk of the search had passed the canyons he must cross. If Bentley could have ridden he would have pulled out with Harris, but while the hip was better, he could not walk nor sit a saddle for any length of time.

Dude left water, the remains of the beans and most of the jerked meat where Bentley could reach them and at full dark started down the east side of the mountain. He let the horse pick its way at its own pace. The last thing he wanted was for it to slip and sprain or break a leg.

The stars were faint, far away, and he saw them only in glimpses through the aspens that grew close on both sides of the trace. Off in the brush an occasional night animal made noise as his passage disturbed it, but he heard nothing more ominous.

Somewhat after three he dropped into a shallow canyon that took him down to the rim of the badlands and for three miles the horse's hoofs clicked on the volcanic rock as they wove between the jagged upthrusts. Then the way straightened and began the long climb toward the plateau where the crumbling buildings of Luck's Bluff stood.

At daylight Harris was still ten miles short of the old town but he judged that he was far enough north that the chance of running into a search party was very slim. He pushed on at an easy gallop that would not tire the horse too much. He would rest it at the Bluff through the day and return to the mountain on the coming night.

In time the old buildings appeared, the slanting headframe of the mine, the smelter where the ore had been treated, then the row of stores and unpainted houses where the miners had lived. At its peak Luck's Bluff had had a population of four thousand. Now it had one single citizen, Jake Babcock.

Through the boom days Babcock had run the company store, hotel and saloon, and when the town died he stayed on. He did not own the buildings but the mine owners had abandoned them and no one questioned his squatter's rights. He kept the store open for the small hill ranchers who found it more convenient to trade there than make the long trip to the Crossing.

Dude had known him for years and never liked him very much. There was a shiftiness about him, he seldom looked directly at you, so Harris was a little surprised, when he tied up at the shaky hitch rail and went inside, that the shriveled little man welcomed him with a grin.

212

"Heard you'd left the country, Dude. Glad to see you didn't."

Dude's nod was indifferent. "Need some supplies, Jake." He began naming what he wanted and Babcock's nose twitched as the list grew longer.

"You got the money to pay for all that? I heard you took off from the Crossing without going near the bank."

Dude laid the ruby ring on the counter and said sourly, "You can keep that until you're better paid. It's worth two thousand dollars."

The storekeeper picked it up, noted the weight of the heavy mounting but complained, "How do I know it's real?"

"It's real. But if you want to argue I'll just take what we need." Dude lifted his gun and leveled it on the man.

Babcock's thin mouth snarled but he said, "I'll keep the ring," and turned to gather the items on the counter.

Over the roar of the river Dude did not hear the sounds outside. Movement on the street was his first warning. Half a dozen horses were wheeling in before the store. Dude spun, hunting a place to hide, then Babcock's voice snapped at him.

"Stand real still, Dude."

Dude swung back, his hand dropping to the butt of his gun, then he froze. Babcock had a double-barreled Greening aimed at his chest.

Dude swore at him. "Put that damn thing away or I'll kill you."

The muzzle did not waver a fraction and an ugly grin showed Babcock's snaggle teeth. The smug voice said,

"You ain't ever going to kill anybody again, Harris. That's Boss Herbert coming in. Him and some riders have been dropping by every few days. He knowed sooner or later you'd run out of grub and this is about the only place you'd likely come for it."

Dude Harris knew what his chances were now, and as close to pleading as he had ever been was in his tone. "Jake, put the gun down. Let me at least take Boss with me."

"The hell I will. You're worth one thousand bucks to me, and Bentley is worth five when he comes looking for you."

And then it was too late. Boss Herbert tramped in with Joe Garvey and four riders on his heels, crossed to Dude and yanked his gun out of the holster, saying,

"Good job, Jake . . . Dude, there's just one way to keep yourself alive. Where's Bentley?"

"Go to hell."

Herbert hit him with a blow from the shoulder. Dude staggered back, crashed against the wall and slid down it, stunned. Joe Garvey passed Herbert, bent to get a handful of Dude's shirt and hauled him up, held him against the boards, grating,

"Mind your manners old man. When Mr. Herbert speaks to you answer him, and say 'Sir' while you're doing it."

Dude spat in the foreman's face. If he was going to die he preferred to be killed quickly. Joe Garvey's rage boiled up and his hand snapped toward his gun, but even as he touched it Boss Herbert roared at him.

"No."

He was beside Garvey, taking the gun, shoving him away, staring him down until the man's eyes dropped and he shook himself under control, then Herbert turned his back and faced Dude.

"Where is he?"

Dude braced himself to keep his feet and spat again. Herbert hit him and his head cracked against the wall. Only his hat kept his skull from breaking.

"Take him outside, boys. Maybe he'll talk better with a rope around his neck."

Two riders grabbed Dude's arms, holding on with both hands as Dude fought them, wrenched the arms up behind Harris's back bent him double and rushed him at a stumbling run through the front door, off the porch and under the tree that shaded the store. A third rider brought a coil of rope from his saddle, shook it out and tossed one end over a lower limb, built a noose and dropped it over Dude's head, pulling it snug. Herbert and Garvey came out, stopping in front of Harris and Herbert's voice clubbed at him.

"Where?"

Dude's mouth was dry but he dragged up enough saliva to spit a third time, but the shot fell short, landing ineffectually in the dust. Herbert clamped a hand on Garvey's shoulder to hold him back and told the man with the rope,

"Haul him up a little, Cliff."

Cliff hauled on the rope. Dude flung himself forward, yanking it out of the man's hand. The two holding him let go of his arms, jumped for the rope and pulled on it. Dude reached up with both hands, caught the rope above his head and dragged himself up it, gasping a breath. Herbert swore heavily and ordered Dude lowered, his hands tied behind him. The rope was slacked off and all three riders climbed on Dude, wrestled him to the ground where two of them fought the writing body until the third had the wrists fastened.

"Now," Herbert said, "take him up again."

The rope was tossed over the limb again and pulled until Dude swung in a slow turn, his toes touching the ground but barely supporting him.

"Last chance, Harris. Tell me where Bentley is."

Dude could not have told them if he had wanted to. He was choking. A black haze in his eyes was blinding him. He did not know who he was facing but he thrust out his tongue. It was swelling in his mouth anyway.

"Take him a little higher."

Cliff said across his shoulder, "He'll strangle."

"Take him up."

Dude was pulled a foot off the ground.

"Now bring him down, loosen the noose."

Dude's feet touched the ground. The men let go of the rope and he fell, limp, and lay without moving.

"Throw a bucket of water on him."

They brought water from the trough. Three buckets one after another. None of them revived him. Dude Harris was dead.

CHAPTER
TWENTY

Cal Bentley did not expect Dude back at the camp until the morning after the second night. When he had not come by the third morning Bentley was not worried. A lot of things could have delayed him, having to detour a search party or lie low until one passed. It was even possible that Babcock was out of the things they needed and Dude had ridden on the sixty miles further north to Rippon.

If that was the case he should come in by the end of the fourth night. But that day passed, and the fifth night came and still there was no Dude. Bentley's concern grew as the dark hours passed.

The hip was much improved. An ugly mottled purple and green bruise still covered it but he could walk and his fear of a bone chip or break was gone. If Dude did not turn up by morning Cal decided he would go look for him. He had only food enough left for one scant meal anyway and could not sit where he was and starve.

The new day came and passed with dragging hours. At sundown Bentley ate the last of the beans, saddled the horse, tucked his rifle in the boot and gingerly lifted to the saddle, gritting at the sharp pain as he eased the injured leg up and over, twisting to the side to take what weight he could off the hip.

He followed the same trail Dude had taken. Harris would use it coming back and they might meet somewhere along it. Only the scurrying animals broke the night quiet. Dawn broke over the land and Bentley rode through the increasing light, his foreboding growing with every mile. He had seen no one by the time he reached the plateau and went forward toward the Bluff. Nothing moved within his sight.

He came into the main street and hauled the horse to a sudden stop. Ahead of him a body swayed on a rope under the tree beside the store, the neck stretched to an incredible length. Bentley knew before he was close enough to identify it.

He stared, not believing. With all his worry he had not expected this. Dude was too careful a man to ride into a trap. But there he was, swinging in slow turns with the gentle breeze.

Bentley went berserk, pulling his colts, spurring at the store. He slid off the horse, ignoring the pain that stabbed through him and without bothering to tie the horse ran across the porch and burst through the door, sweeping the room with a wild stare. Babcock was alone, just coming from the rear storeroom. Under the thunder of the river he had not heard Bentley's pounding steps and he froze for a moment, then edged along behind the counter, never taking his eyes off Bentley and the gun in his hand. Bentley shouted at him.

"What happened?"

Babcock ran a pale tongue that was suddenly too dry around his shriveled lips. "They . . . They sneaked up while he was ordering grub. Busted in here before either of us saw them."

"And Herbert hung him." It came as a choked cry.

"They didn't mean to kill him, just scare him into saying where you was, but something went wrong and he strangled." As he talked Babcock moved along the counter, then stopped and reached under it. "Here's the ring he . . ."

"Get back." Bentley's voice was a whip crack. It made Babcock jump.

"Don't you want it?"

"Move off from there, ten feet."

Reluctantly the storekeeper moved, his eyes fastened on Bentley's gun. Cal walked around the counter, saw the Greening beneath it on the shelf and picked it up, shaking it at the man.

"You pulled this on Dude. You threw down on him so Herbert could take him. Damn you . . ."

"So help me . . ."

"Don't lie like that. You turned him in. If you hadn't been in on it Herbert would never have left you alive to tell what they did." Bentley was screaming in his rage. "How long has he hung there? Why didn't you cut him down? Why haven't you . . . A trap for me."

Carrying both his gun and the shotgun Bentley whirled to run for the door, but before he made it there were horses driving up the street. He spun and dashed toward the storeroom that backed up at the edge of the bluff above the river.

Boots drummed across the porch as Bentley slammed the door, hearing Babcock's yell.

"He's in there . . . back there . . ."

Bentley threw three heavy cases against the panel, sent a shotgun blast through it, then raced to the single window, broke out the glass with the gun butt and had a fleeting glance at the rushing water far below. He shoved his colts in the holster as bullets from the store splintered the door, fired the second barrel of the Greening and flung himself through the window.

It seemed to him that he fell a mile before he splashed into the rushing Whitewater and went deep. The current dragged him downstream at a freight train speed. He was thrown to the surface as the deep water sluiced up over a rock and had one gasping breath before he was pulled under again, rolled over and over, torn at, swept along. He held his breath until he was tossed up again, sucked in air and swam with the current, fighting to keep on top.

The Whitewater here had an infamous name. Men who had fallen into it seldom survived and some bodies had never been found. Those that were, were broken on the rocks of the rapids downstream.

Bentley was shot between the high cliff walls as if through a hose. They spun over him dizzily as the torrent pounded him like heavy hammers. Then far downstream the rush slowed, the river widened and he was through the sluice, being swung in whirling eddies, then into a boiling backwash behind a reef of boulders. Hardly conscious, he became vaguely aware of rubbing against pebbles and sand, then he was washed around the swirl again before he could react. The second circle took him against the grit again and more by instinct than will he clawed into it, dragging himself up it until he lay half out of water on a spit of ground.

He sagged there, the pull of water tugging at his legs, the roar of the sluice above engulfing him in a world of roaring sound. Finally he roused enough to roll, to pull his legs under him and sit up, haunted by a nagging feeling that there was something he must do.

It came to him slowly through the fog in his mind. Boss Herbert and the crew would be riding the canyon rim just to make certain he had not escaped from the grip of the river.

He looked about. At the land end of the bar a small undercut had been gouged out of the cliff at some time of higher water. It was only about two feet deep but it was cave enough to conceal him from sight from above. It was there, but could he get to it? The bar was more than fifteen feet long and strewn with rock. He tried to stand but his legs would not hold him up and he sank back, settling for crawling on hands and knees. It seemed to take an hour before he curled into the shelter and the effort took the last of his strength.

He slept. Some time later voices roused him, shouting above the water noise, and he knew that the Box H was close above his head.

The sounds grew faint, then died. Bentley sank into sleep again and the next time he waked morning light was just hitting the top of the western cliff. For a moment he was befuddled, then he knew that he had slept through the last afternoon and the night.

He squirmed out of the cave and stood up carefully. The hip hurt and he was stiff and sore throughout his body. He walked painfully out on the bar to study the wall above. It was impossible to climb it from where he stood, bare rock and leaned toward the river, the rim overhanging it by two feet. He followed it downstream with his eyes and found no place that offered hope. Unless he could find a way up he was faced with two choices, sit here until he starved or again risk the terrible power of the Whitewater.

He looked upstream. For a hundred feet the wall was sheer and unbroken. Then he saw the crevice, a narrow crack running upward, dug by flash floods pouring over the edge. Whether he could get to it was a question, but it was his only chance except the river and the turbulent rapids between where he was and the valley.

He brought his attention down to the water, studying the patterns of the swirls as they swung in against the cliff. If it was shallow enough he might walk through the water but he would have to fight the current.

Cautiously he stepped into it, feeling his way with his feet, digging his fingernails into the face for what little grip he could find, moving step by careful step. The tugging current dragged at his legs, then his waist, then his chest, and at that depth lifted him and wheeled him back to the bar.

He sat down, resting from the battle, thinking, then got up, walked to the outer edge of the swirling pattern and stepped into it there. It carried him up toward the main stream and he floated on it until it curved around toward the cliff, then he thrashed out, swimming across the whorl as it carried him around. He came against the bank near the upstream edge, grabbed at the rough wall, and with his body horizontal in the water clawed hand over hand until he caught the edge of the crevice.

He found a foothold in it under the surface and thrust up, reaching for a purchase higher, then another, and with that was free of the drag.

The cliff was only forty feet tall but it took an hour of inching up, clinging like a fly in the fissure, afraid that at any second the tuft of growth or the protruding stone to which he gave his weight would pull loose and drop him. Then he was at the rim, reaching for the tough branch of a bush hanging over the edge, easing on up and at last bending over the top and squirming his hips onto the solid ground.

He crawled on, under the bush and lay while his muscles quivered for half an hour and his strength built up again. Then he got up and started walking. Back toward Luck's Bluff. He did not know how far downstream he had been swept but certainly the old mining camp was closer than anything else.

Too, his horse was there unless Herbert had taken it with him. Food was there and what he needed even more, a gun, for the river had taken his.

He walked steadily all morning and into midafternoon before he saw the abandoned buildings. He was tired, but it was caution rather than fatigue that made him approach with slow care. There were no horses at the rail, no sign of anyone along the street, but Dude's body still swung to remind him of danger.

He passed it, keeping to the sidewalk close to the wall and stepped silently to the porch, avoiding a broken step, and stopped beside the open door to peer around the jamb. Babcock was not in sight. No one else was. Bentley ran quietly behind the counter, found the Greening that had been replaced there and took it up with a sigh. He felt far better with that in his hands. He shouted.

"Babcock."

The storeroom door was opened and the man put his head out.

"What's wante . . . ?"

The word cut off and the storekeeper goggled at the apparition, then he croaked, "You're dead."

"No. But you will be if you give me any trouble. Where's my horse?"

The man swallowed and put a shaking hand to his throat. "In the corral. How . . . ?"

"Get me a short gun, and be very careful how you handle it."

Babcock sidled to a roll-top desk, unlocked and opened it and picked up a heavy gun by the barrel, held it out in front of him as he brought it to the counter and laid it there. It might have been a snake. Bentley helped himself to a box of shells without taking his eyes off Babcock.

"Now the ruby."

The storekeeper hesitated. Bentley leveled the Greening higher. Babcock felt in a pocket, brought out the ring and dropped it beside the gun, his eyes bright with hatred.

With the shotgun locked under his arm and his finger on the trigger Bentley broke the short gun and shoved shells in one handed, then dropped it in the holster, picked up the ring.

"Now get a shovel and a wheelbarrow. You're going to cut Dude down and bury him."

The old man moved slowly, limping, as if age and infirmity would win him sympathy. Bentley had none for him. He prodded the bent back with the shotgun barrel and marched him to the corner where tools were stacked, then to the yard for the barrow. While Bentley stood back Babcock set the barrow under Dude, cut the rope to drop him into it, then wheeled the body to the overgrown cemetery and dug the grave.

When the burial was finished Bentley walked Babcock to the corral, ordered him to saddle the horse, noting with satisfaction that his rifle was still in the boot, then he swung up.

"Where do I find Boss Herbert and Joe Garvey?"

Babcock was too cowed for evasion. "I'm not sure," he said, "but Boss told Garvey to take the men to your place and start rounding up the cattle you turned loose."

"Where did Boss go?"

"Back to the Crossing to tell Able Allen you were dead."

"Some advice, Babcock. You've seen I'm hard to kill. Don't get any idea about telling Herbert I'm alive or I'll come back and throw you off that cliff and we'll see how you like shooting the river."

As he started out of the corral Babcock called, "Hey . . .That's my Greening . . ."

"Was your Greening. I don't want to be shot in the back."

Bentley rode off in the fading day, watchful but letting his mind drift back over the years with Dude Harris. The memories were many and it hurt deeply that there would be no more. He rode doggedly through the night and he was many miles away when hunger broke through his consciousness. He had eaten nothing since he left the mountain camp and there had been too much of shock, of escape, of burning fixation on Boss Herbert to leave room for thoughts of food. But now it was closer to his own ranch than it was back to Luck's Bluff, so he rode on.

It was noon again when he scouted the foot of his canyon, saw no one and turned up it. At the natural gate he left his horse, took the rifle and went ahead on foot. Smoke rose from the chimney. He went carefully until he could see the corrals. There were no cattle in the big one and only one horse in the smaller.

One man inside. He hardly dared hope it would be Joe Garvey but as he came around the rear corner the foreman opened the kitchen door and came out, heading for the well. His head snapped around and he jarred to a stop. They stood not ten feet apart.

Neither spoke. After his first moment of surprise Garvey was like a coiled spring. His hand shot toward the holster at his hip but his clawing fingers never touched the gun butt. Bentley shot him in the chest once, once in the head, and watched the man collapse almost at his feet.

Bentley bolted past the body into the house. There were beans simmering on the stove, a pan of biscuits reheating and coffee in the pot. He did not know where Garvey's crew was, out looking for cows he supposed, possibly near enough to have heard the shots, and they would be coming for the noon meal soon.

Still, he had to eat. He wolfed some beans, drained a coffee cup and poured the biscuits into a pocket, then he looked outside, saw no one coming and ran for his horse.

CHAPTER
TWENTY-ONE

Able Allen was at his kitchen table having a lonely evening snack. For the most part he took his meals at the hotel, but as the word had spread that Dude Harris and Cal Bentley were dead people coming to the bank had pestered him with questions about details that Boss Herbert had given him. He had been able to shut most of the curious out of his office but at the hotel dining room he would be open prey, so he had made himself a sandwich and coffee to enjoy in privacy.

He heard the front door open and assumed Beth Herbert was there. She had the habit of dropping by when he did not appear downtown. He called a welcome, heard steps in the hall, and the next second was looking at the ghost of Cal Bentley.

Allen did not believe in ghosts. He was frozen, staring in disbelief.

Bentley's live voice said, "Able, you are under arrest for dynamiting the jail and killing Josh Roebuck."

Allen sank against the chair, shaking, then returning confidence made him laugh silently. "You damned fool, coming back to town. Everybody thought you were dead, but now Boss Herbert and Joe Garvey and the whole crew will be swarming over you again."

228

"Garvey's dead."

Allen was jarred again and his voice came strained. "What do you mean . . . How?"

"He tried to draw on me. I beat him to it."

The banker drew a long, ragged breath. The wits that he depended on to talk himself out of tight situations might as well be locked in his safe at this moment and he could only fall back on a banal bluster, saying weakly.

"You know you can't get away with that."

"I've already killed Garvey and in one minute I'll kill you unless you sign a confession. You will write that you blasted the jail, are responsible for the death of Josh Roebuck and that Boss Herbert told you he had hung Dude Harris. Get it all down. Now."

Allen sat very still for a long moment, then his right hand darted inside his coat. Before it disappeared Bentley had his short gun pointed at the man. The hand stopped and stayed out of sight. Allen whispered hoarsely,

"I need paper to write on, don't I? It's in my inside pocket."

"I'll get it. Bring your hand out empty and put both of them on the table."

Allen obeyed slowly, spreading his hands far apart on the table top, clenched to hide their shaking. Bentley moved in behind him, reached over his shoulder and folded the lapel back. He first took out the little ladies' gun, so light that it did not disturb the hang of the coat, and threw it across the room, then felt again for the folded sheet of paper and the precisely sharpened

229

pencil, dropped them before Allen and touched the back of his neck with the cold metal of his Colt's barrel.

"Write."

Bentley watched the man take up the pencil and begin making hen scratches on the paper, his fingers trembling.

"Make it legible."

Pale-faced and with sweat standing in beads on his forehead, Allen began again, his effort like that of a child just learning to form his letters. Bentley watched coldly. His goals were falling into place but he had paid a dear price. If he had not been so determined that the dam project succeed Dude Harris would be alive. So would Sally's father. And he could hope to see her again.

Able Allen put his name at the bottom of the paper. Bentley told him to stand up and when he was on his feet Cal put the paper in his pocket and motioned Allen toward the front door. The banker moved in a daze, out of his house and down the street ahead of Bentley, Cal carrying his rifle but holstering the short gun. It was the supper hour and no one saw them pass.

There was light in the jail and Bentley asked Allen who would be there and had a dull answer that Brandy Ives and his old deputies had been reappointed. At the door Bentley sent Allen in first and stepped in close behind him.

Ives was behind the desk, his chair tipped back and his feet up on the corner. The deputies were not there. The front legs of the chair came down with a crashing thud and the sheriff half rose, stopped and settled back, his eyes bugging on Bentley.

"You . . . ?"

Bentley moved away from the door, closed it and prodded the banker to the desk.

"I have just arrested Able Allen for murder, Brandy."

Ives gaped from one to the other, his face turning deep red and his chin thrusting out.

"You can't arrest nobody anymore. I'm sheriff again and I'll say who is and who ain't arrested in my town."

"Read this." Bentley spread the confession on the desk and Ives picked it up unwillingly, read, and dropped the paper as though it burned his fingers.

"How did you get this?"

Allen said with sudden hope, "At the point of a gun. That's a crime, Brandy."

"I'll say it is. Cal, you got no right to do that even if you was sher . . ."

Bentley cut him short, his voice stone hard. "While you were wearing out the seat of your pants here Herbert and Garvey hung Dude Harris at Luck's Bluff and tried to kill me. I took care of Garvey and . . ."

"You what?"

"He tried to draw on me at my place. I shot him."

Brandy Ives was looking at Bentley as if he had never seen him before, as if he were being threatened himself. His small red tongue circled his lips and his voice had a hollow, uncertain sound.

"What would you do if I tried to lock you up for killing Joe Garvey?"

"What do you think?"

"That's what I was afraid of." The sheriff squirmed tighter against the chair seat to make it plain he had no intention of challenging this hard faced stranger. "I never believed any man had the guts to stand up toe to toe to Boss . . ."

Bentley found a half smile for the man. He wanted cooperation and he eased off his harshness.

"Somebody finally had to, it finally dawned on me. Colonel Ruggles and I made the mistake of believing that in beating him legally we had won the fight. I found out that Herbert respects nothing but violence, so I'll give him violence."

Brandy Ives's breath sucked in. "You mean to kill him too?"

"I mean to arrest him and let the law execute him."

"The Box H will never let you do that."

Cal Bentley was getting very weary of the old sheriff's refusal to do the job he was being paid for and he said sharply,

"We'll see. Now lock Allen in that cell."

Ives looked at the banker, seeing beyond him the shadow of the man who had held him and everyone else in fief for so many years and the habit of fear was too strong for him. He shook his head, saying quickly,

"I'll have nothing to do with it."

"Brandy, don't make me get rough with you. Lock him up and give me the key. Then you can do anything you want. Leave town if you like."

A deep shuddering sigh came from the man as he got heavily to his feet and jerked his head at Allen without meeting the banker's eyes.

232

"I like. I'll have to."

He plodded to the cell, opened it and stood aside and Able Allen with Bentley on his heels walked in. Ives locked the grille and held the key toward Bentley, then dropped his empty hand to his side as if it weighed a ton.

Bentley pocketed the key and asked, "You any idea where Boss is now? Where the crew is?"

There was no life in the answering voice. "He had supper at the hotel. I'd guess he's playing poker or blackjack there. Crew's all out hunting the cattle you ran off."

Bentley backed across the office, the rifle half raised in his hands. He did not believe Brandy Ives would shoot him in the back but he was not going to give him the opportunity. Brandy understood and his face clouded with hurt. He might not be the bravest sheriff in the country but he would not have resorted to shooting a man down who wasn't looking.

At the door Bentley stepped out, closed it behind him and ran along the dark sidewalk toward his last appointment with Dude Harris's murderers.

CHAPTER
TWENTY-TWO

The street door of the saloon was at the front of the long room. When Boss Herbert played cards he always sat with his shoulders against the rear wall so that he could see everything that happened in the place. The moment Bentley came through that door Herbert would see him and all chance of surprise would be lost.

He could go in with his gun in his hand but Herbert would probably draw even so and he would have to kill the rancher. That was not what he wanted. He wanted to arrest the man, to see him tried and convicted. He wanted the state to execute Boss because only in that way could the people of the Crossing reclaim their repect for the law.

The only other entrance to the saloon was through the lobby door halfway down the room and if the usual crowd of men standing around the tables to watch the play of those seated were there, Bentley might be able to slip through them and get close to Herbert before Boss discovered him.

He crossed the hotel porch and went through the wide double door and saw Beth Herbert with her embroidery, her head bowed over it, living out the weeks here since he had burned the Box H ranch and tonight, he knew, expecting that it soon would be rebuilt.

He kept his face averted, hoping that she would not look up, and headed for the arch. But he heard her gasp, heard her boots scrape the floor, heard her gasp his name in a whisper that carried through the lobby. There was nothing for it but to go on. He passed her in three long strides, stood the rifle behind the desk, pulled his short gun and stepped into the saloon, easing among the watchers.

He was intent on getting close to Herbert to knock him out with the heavy barrel and drag him unconscious to jail. Any other way would mean a gunfight. He was moving well, no one was paying any attention to him. His path took him across toward the bar and he had reached that when Beth Herbert's scream came behind him, telling her father to watch out.

Herbert's head came up from the cards he was playing. He saw Bentley, froze for the barest instant then slammed to his feet, kicking the table out of his way. Money and chips and the four other players scattered, the men falling and staying down as Herbert clawed at his gun. The rancher's reflexes were fast.

Bentley leveled his Colts. It was going to have to be himself or Herbert, but perhaps he could shoot the man's shoulder without killing him. Before he could fire a pair of arms were flung around him, pulling him off balance.

He knew who it was, would have known even without the perfume that was so much a part of her. Beth Herbert had worn the scent for years.

He cursed and tried to break her grip, seeing Herbert's gun come up and knew that in an instant the big finger would squeeze away the shot. He tried to throw himself sideways to spoil the aim but his body hit the bar and he was spun around, the girl clinging to him, dragged around with him. Beth Herbert's back was flung into the line of fire at the exact time the cattleman's gun exploded.

Bentley felt the jar of her body against him, heard the air driven from her and felt the arms loosen as she slid away from him. His first shot covered Herbert's second and a bullet whipped past his ear. He saw his bullet strike the center of Herbert's shirt and throw out a tiny spurt of dust. Then lead crashed into Bentley's shoulder and knocked him in a spinning fall to the splintered floor just beyond the crumpled body of the girl.

He was conscious but the shock of the blow had paralyzed his muscles. He saw Herbert's feet come toward him, saw them stop, braced apart beside the girl, then Herbert dropped to his knees and buried his big head against his daughter's body and his sobs rasped out her name again and again. With an anguished howl Boss Herbert was lifted and thrust forward to fall across the girl, collapsed.

Hands reached to turn him over, roll him off her and an amazed sound grunted from those closest. Boss Herbert was dead.

236

Bentley's bullet had struck close to the heart. The wonder was that the cattleman had crossed the distance to the bar, a dead man walking was the way Doc Morey said it some days later.

"I wouldn't believe it if I hadn't heard it from so many who saw it," Morey marveled. "It just goes to prove that when a man is stubborn enough he can even shove death away for a few minutes. Funny thing. Apparently he didn't realize he'd bit Beth until he got to her, must have thought you'd just knocked her down. When he saw the blood on her back, saw she was dead he just let go, quit. He thought the world of that girl, only human being he ever cared about."

"I'm sure of that," Bentley said from the hotel bed. His shoulder was tightly bandaged and throbbed with pain. "What's happened with Able Allen?"

"Brandy still has him in jail. He'll be tried for killing Josh Roebuck . . . which reminds me . . . here's a letter that came yesterday from the Roebuck girl. You want me to read it to you?"

"Please." His loss of blood had so weakened him that he knew he could not hold the paper.

Dear Cal:
I just read in the Denver paper how you had been shot and am writing Doc Morey to find out how bad it is. Yes, we came back to Denver. I decided I had made a mistake, that if you want me, why, I'll go any place you say. Let me know. You never said it but I thought you loved me, and I know I love you. Sally.

Bentley lay against the pillow smiling. Her forthrightness was one of the things he loved most about her.

"Write her, Doc. Say I want her very much. Tell her the dam is going to be built and her people can have jobs and take up land the way they intended."

"I already did," Morey told him. "Mailed a letter right back."

Cal Bentley's head came around sharply. "But . . . ?"

"How'd I know you'd want me to? I've watched you a long time, Cal . . . Ever since I slapped you when you first came into this world."